No More / C'est Tout

MARGUERITE DURAS

translated by
RICHARD HOWARD

afterword by
CHRISTIANE BLOT-LABAREERE

SEVEN STORIES PRESS
NEW YORK ∗ OAKLAND ∗ LONDON

Seven Stories Press
140 Watts Street
New York, NY 10013
sevenstories.com

Library of Congress Cataloging-in-Publication Data

Names: Duras, Marguerite, author. | Howard, Richard, 1929- translator. | Duras, Marguerite. C'est tout. | Duras, Marguerite. C'est tout. English.

Title: No more = C'est tout / Marguerite Duras ; translated from the French by Richard Howard.
Other titles: C'est tout
Description: Seven Stories Press first edition. | New York : Seven Stories Press, 2022.
Identifiers: LCCN 2022014288 | ISBN 9781644212394 (trade paperback)
Subjects: LCSH: Duras, Marguerite--Translations into English. | LCGFT: Literature. | Diaries.
Classification: LCC PQ2607.U8245 C413 2022 | DDC 843/.912--dc23/eng/20221019
LC record available at https://lccn.loc.gov/2022014288

Printed in the USA.

9 8 7 6 5 4 3 2 1

For Yann.
You never know, before,
what you are writing.
Think of me: lose no time.

For Yann, my lover of the night.
Signed: Marguerite, the lover of
her beloved, November 20, 1994
Paris, rue Saint-Benoît.

CONTENTS

TRANSLATOR'S NOTE

It was Chateaubriand who initiated a literature explicitly from the other side, posthumous writing, *d'outre-tombe.* There are subsequent French instances—Drieu La Rochelle's *Récit secret,* Gide's mortuary pillow-book *Ainsi soit-il,* some late Jouhandeau, quite a lot of Montherlant, perhaps Céline's last three volumes—the mere instancing of these ominous names suggests the ethical risk of such an enterprise. Who makes book here—isn't there always someone else, someone not entirely to be trusted who will have to collect the *disjecta verba,* to straighten things out—in Duras's case her last young lover, appearing so mysteriously as a gruesome interlocutor, the angel of death masked as the last coital gasp, drowning out all foregoing competition during these inter-comatose manifestations of that special literary fanaticism which asserts not merely that *this is happening* (after all, Duras has written a hundred works, novels, stories, plays, films; expression is her trade) but that *this is happening to me!*

No attempt will be made to please, to beguile the (loathed?) reader. Nor to identify anything so trivial as circumstance. We are in the abstract—and perhaps fraudulently dated—halls of Dis where only glints of consciousness, when they come, will suffice: angry, dismissive, these are the intermittences not of the heart, as in Proust, but of the spleen. Baudelaire indeed is the plausible prototype, though what scorn M.D. would have for all his formal scruples, his attention to the classicism of ruin. Here is nothing but what the French call *hargne* (surliness, resentment, bad temper . . .), tense and often mocking observations of the still-articulate soul, betrayed by the still-longing body. This is one of the fiercest little books in our culture, the converse of the Stoic manual of *proper dying*. Give it the last inch on your bedside table to remind you (like the slave whose function it is to slap the victorious Roman general before he sets out on his Triumphal March) of the degradations of mortality: greedy, illicit, profound. *Odi et amo.*

—RICHARD HOWARD
Spring 1998
New York City

RICHARD HOWARD (1929–2022) was an acclaimed translator and poet. His poetry collection Untitled Subjects won the 1970 Pulitzer Prize, and his translation of Baudelaire's Les Fleurs du mal won the American Book Award in 1983.

FOREWORD

It was toward the end of August 1995 that Yann Andréa brought me the beginnings of *C'est Tout:* a few typed sheets which went from November 20, 1994 to August 1, 1995. We published them right away, and Marguerite Duras was able to see the book. Everyone knew at the time that she was mortally ill. Then a few days after her death on March 3, 1996, Yann gave me the pages which end on February 29. In the notes she herself wrote or in those retranscribed by Yann, the striking thing, for anyone who knew Marguerite Duras toward the end of her life, is that immediately recognizable voice, her outrageous and powerful way of forcing the language to obey her thought, a way which has here become lapidary, on account of the urgency of the message and the fear of silence. She spoke exactly as she wrote, or the other way around. It is for what they say, and also for her will to speak to the very end, that I find these pages—poorly typed on an old machine, not even an electric typewriter—so overwhelming. And also because the whole of her work is to be found in them, in fragments and flashes and echoes, as always reworked and revisited, this ultimate time, truly the last.

—PAUL OTCHAKOVSKY-LAURENS
Spring 1998
Paris, France

PAUL OTCHAKOVSKY-LAURENS (1944–2018) was the publisher of P.O.L in Paris. Duras befriended him late in her career and chose him to publish her final works.

No More

November 21, afternoon, rue Saint-Benoît.

Y.A.: What would you say for yourself?
M.D.: Duras.
Y.A.: What would you say for me?
M.D.: Unintelligible.

Later, the same afternoon.

Sometimes I am empty for a very long time.
I have no identity.
At first it is frightening. And then it
turns to an impulse of happiness. And then it stops.
Happiness: I mean dead, somewhat.
Somewhat missing from the place where I am speaking.

Later still.

It is a question of time. I shall
write a book.

I want to, but it's not certain I am
writing this book.
It is aleatory.

November 22, afternoon, rue Saint-Benoît.

Y.A.: Are you afraid of death?
M.D.: I don't know. I don't know how to
answer. I don't know anything anymore
since I've reached the sea.
Y.A.: And with me?
M.D.: Before and now it is love between us, between you and
me.
Death and love. It will be whatever you want, whatever you
are.
Y.A.: Your definition of yourself?
M.D.: I don't know, just as right now
I don't know what to write.
Y.A.: Which of your books do you prefer to all the rest?
M.D.: *The Sea Wall,* childhood.

Y.A.: And you'll go to paradise?
M.D.: No. That makes me laugh.
Y.A.: Why?
M.D.: I don't know. I don't believe in
such a thing.
Y.A.: And after death, what's left?
M.D.: Nothing. Except the living who smile, who remember.

Y.A.: Who will remember you?
M.D.: Young readers. Students.

Y.A.: What is on your mind?
M.D.: Writing. A tragic occupation, at least in relation to the
course of life.
I am in that without effort.

Later, the same afternoon.

Y.A.: Do you have a title for the next book?
M.D.: Yes. The vanishing act.

November 23 in Paris, 3 in the afternoon.

I want to talk about someone.
About a man of twenty-five
at the most.
He is a beautiful man who wants
to die before being marked by
death.
You loved him.
More than that.

The beauty of his hands,
Yes, that's right.
His hands which move forward with
the hill—distinct now, bright,
as luminous as a child's
grace.
I kiss you.
I wait for you the way I wait for
someone who will destroy this failed
grace, gentle and still warm.
Given to you, wholly, with my whole
body, this grace.

Later the same afternoon.

I wanted to tell you
that I loved you.
To shout it.
No more.

Rue Saint-Benoît, Sunday, November 27.

Being together is love,
death, speaking, sleeping.

Later, that Sunday.

Y.A.: What do you have to say about yourself?
M.D.: I am no longer quite sure who
I am.
I am with my lover.
The name: I don't know.
It is not important.
To be together as with a
lover.
I would have liked that to happen to me.
To be together with a lover.

Silence, and then.

Y.A.: What use is writing?
M.D.: It's a way of keeping still and speaking
at the same time. Writing. And that means
singing sometimes.
Y.A.: Dancing?
M.D.: That counts too. It's a condition
of the individual, dancing. I used to
love dancing.
Y.A.: Why?
M.D.: I don't know yet.

Silence, and then.

Y.A.: Are you very gifted?
M.D.: Yes, it seems to me that I am.

Writing is very close to the rhythm
of speech.

Monday, November 28, 3 in the afternoon, rue Saint-Benoît.

Something must be said about the man in
The Malady of Death.
Who is he:
How did he manage to get here?
Write about emaciation,
starting with the emaciation of a man.

Another day.

He has not reappeared in the
bedroom.
Never.
It was no use waiting for his singing,
sometimes gay, sometimes sad,
sometimes glum.

How quickly he turned back into the bird
I had known in the fields.

Later, another day (the same one).

Let Yann know that it is not he who writes
the letters, but that he could sign
the last one. That would give me the deepest
pleasure.
Signed: Duras.

Later still.

My lover's Chinese name.
I have never spoken to him in his
language.

Another day, rue Saint-Benoît.

For Yann.
For nothing.
The sky is empty.

For years now I've loved this man.
A man whom I have not yet named.
A man whom I love.
A man who will leave me.
The rest, before, after me,
Ahead and behind me, is a matter
of indifference. I love you.

You can no longer pronounce the name
I bear and given by my parents.
Unknown lovers.
Never mind, whatever you like.
Still a few days more of waiting.
You ask me waiting for what,
I answer: I don't know.
Waiting.
In the wind's transformation.
Maybe tomorrow I shall write you
again.

One can live on that.
Laughing and then crying.
I speak of the time that trickles out of
the earth.
I am out of breath.
I must stop speaking.

Later.

Various activities which tempt me from
time to time, for example the death of
that young man. I no longer know his name,
what to call him. Literally his insignificance
is great.

Silence, and then.

I no longer have the slightest notion about
what I thought I knew or expected to
see again.
There it is, and no more.

Silence, and then.

The beginning of the end of that
really terrifying love,
with the regret for each hour.
And then there was the hour that followed,
incomprehensible, emerging from the depths
of time.
Horrible hour.
Splendid and horrible.

I managed not to kill myself
simply because of the idea of his death.
Of his death and of his life.

Silence, and then.

I haven't said the main thing about his
person, his soul, his feet, his
hands, his laughter.
The main thing for me is to
abandon his gaze when he is alone.
When he is in the disorder of
thought.
He is very beautiful. It is hard to know.
If I begin speaking of him, I
never stop.
My life is somehow uncertain, more
uncertain, yes, than his life
before me.

Silence, and then.

I'd like to go on digressing
the way I do on certain summer
afternoons like this one.

I no longer have the taste for it
nor the courage.

October 14, 1994.

October 14, 1914. Here the title means
nothing except for the author. The title
means nothing then. The title too awaits
that: a title. A cement.
I am on the verge of the fatal date.
It is VOID.
Yet the date is written on
pale paper.
It has been written by a man's
blond head.
A child's head.
Myself, I believe this: I believe
beyond myself what has been written
parallel to this child's head.
It is the REMAINDER of the writing.
It is a meaning of the writing.
It is also the scent of a love
which proceeded here, with the child.
A love without direction
redolent of a child's flesh a child
dying to read what is unknown about desire. Everything will
collapse when the
text to be read is erased.

October 15.

l am in contact with myself
in a freedom which coincides with
myself.

Silence, and then.

l never had a model.
l disobeyed by obeying.
When l write l am the same
madness as in life. l join the
rock-mass when l write.
The rocks of the Sea Wall.

Saturday December 10, 3 in the afternoon, rue Saint-Benoît.

You head straight for
solitude.
Not me, l have books.

Silence, and then.

I feel I am lost.
Equivalent to dead.
It is terrifying.
I no longer feel like making the effort.
I think of no one.
The rest is over.
You as well.
I am alone.

Silence, and then.

It is no longer on unhappiness that you
live, it is despair.

Silence, and then.

Y.A.: Who are you?
M.D.: Duras, no more.
Y.A.: What does Duras do?
M.D.: She does literature.

Silence, and then.

Find something more to write.

Paris, December 25, 1994.

The children's rain has fallen
into the sun.
With happiness.
I went to see.
Afterwards, it had to be explained to them
that this was natural. For centuries.
Because the children did not understand,
could not yet understand
the intelligence of the Gods.
Afterward it was necessary to go on
walking in the forest. And singing
with the grown-ups, the dogs, the cats.

Paris, December 28.

A letter for me.
It would be enough to change
or to leave off without any
transformation.
The letter.

December 31, 1994.

Happy New Year to Yann Andréa.
Your short letters bore me.

January 3, rue Saint-Benoît.

Yann, I am still here.
I have to leave.
I no longer know where to go.
I am writing to you as if I were
calling to you.
Perhaps you could see me.
I know this will be no use.

January 6.

Yann.
I hope to see you at the end of the afternoon.
With all my heart.
With all my heart.

February 10.

An intelligence on its way out.
As though escaping.
When someone says the word writer to
Duras, it has a double weight.
I am the wild and unexpected
writer.

Later, the same afternoon.

Vanity of vanities.
All is vanity and pursuit of the
wind.
These two phrases afford
all the literature of the earth.
Vanity of vanities, yes.
These two phrases all by themselves
open the world: things, winds,
children's cries, the sun
dead while these cries are uttered.
Let the world proceed to its ruin.
Vanity of vanities.
All is vanity and pursuit of the
wind.

March 3.

That is what I am, pursuit of the
wind.

Silence, and then.

There are papers I must sort out
in the shadow of my
intelligence.
What I am doing is indelible.

Saturday March 25.

I am upset that the decades
go by so fast. But all the same
I am on this side of the world.
It is so hard to die.
At a certain moment of life,
things are over.
I feel them that way: things
are over.
That is the way it is.

Silence, and then.

I would love you until my death.
I shall try not to die
too soon.
That is all I have to do.

Silence, and then.

Yann, don't you feel you're
a kind of dependency of Duras?

Good Friday.

Take me in your weeping,
in your laughter, in your tears.

Holy Saturday.

What I am going to turn into.
I am afraid.
Come.

Come with me.

Later, the same afternoon.

Let's go see the horror, death.

Later still.

Caress me.
Come into my face with me.
Quick, come.

Silence, and then.

I love you too much.
I can't write any more.
Love too great between us,
even to horror.

Silence, and then.

I don't know where I'm going.
I'm afraid.
Let's take the road together.
Come quick.
I'll send you letters.
No more.
It frightens me to write.
Things like that
frighten me.

April 9. Palm Sunday.

Both of us are innocents.

Silence, and then.

I have a meager life now.
Poor.
I have become poor.
I am going to write a new text.
Without a man. Now there will be nothing.
I am almost nothing now.
I see nothing now.

It is still everything, for a long time,
before death.

Later.

There is no last kiss.

Later still.

You don't have to worry about
the money.
No more.
I have nothing more to say.
Not even a word.
Nothing to say.
Let's go for a little walk along the road.

That same Sunday.

If there is a God, it's you. You

believe in Him as hard as iron, don't you.

Silence, and then.

I can begin all over again.
Starting tomorrow.
At any moment.
I'm beginning a book again.
I'm writing.
And there it is!
I know something about language.
That's something I'm really good at.

Silence, and then.

You know, that's a confirmation of Duras,
everywhere in this world and the next.

Wednesday April 12, afternoon, rue Saint-Benoît.

Come.
Come into the sun, what there is of it.

April 13.

All my life I've written.
Like a sausage out of the grinder,
that's what I've done.
And there's nothing wrong with being
like that.
I've never been pretentious.
Writing your whole life, you learn
to write. It doesn't help at all.

Wednesday April 19, 3 p.m., rue Saint-Benoît.

It turns out I have talent.
I'm used to it now.

Silence, and then.

I'm a stick of wood.
So are you.
Another kind.

June 11.

You are what you are, and that
delights me.

Silence, and then.

Come quick.
Quick, give me a little of your
strength.
Come into my face.

June 28.

The word love exists.

July 3, 3 p.m., Neauphle-le-Château.

I know perfectly well that you have other
ambitions. I know perfectly well that you
are sad. But that doesn't matter to me.
That you love me is the most important thing.

The rest doesn't matter to me. The hell
with it.

Later, the same afternoon.

I feel crushed by existence.
It makes me want to write.
I wrote very well about you when you
left—about the man
whom I love.
You are in the strongest spell
I have ever seen.
You are responsible for everything.
Whatever I've done you could have
done.
I hear you saying that you have given up
this sentence, that sentence.

Silence, and then.

Do you hear this silence.
I hear the sentences you spoke
instead of the woman who is writing.

Silence, and then.

Everything was written by you, by that
body you have.
I'm going to stop this text here and
go on with another by you, made for
you, made instead of you.

Silence, and then.

All right, what would it be, what
you mean by writing?

Silence, and then.

I cannot endure your changing.

July 4 at Neauphle.

Like an immediate fear of
death.
And afterwards an enormous weariness.

Silence, and then.

Come.
We must speak of our love.
We'll find the words for that.
Maybe there will be no words.

Silence, and then.

I love life, even the way it is
here.
It's all right, I've found the words.

Later, the same day.

In the future, I want nothing.
Except to speak more about myself,
all the time, monotonously.
More about myself.

Silence, and then.

I want all this to vanish or
for God to kill me.

Silence, and then.

Come quick.
I feel better.
The fear is less solid.
Leave me here where I am with
my mother's fear of death, remaining
intact, whole.
No more.

Saturday July 8, 2 p.m., at Neauphle.

There's nothing left in my head
but empty things.

Silence, and then.

That does it.
I am a dead woman.

It's over.

Silence, and then.

Tonight we'll have something very strong
to eat. Something Chinese, for instance.
A dish from wrecked China.

July 10, at Neauphle.

You are becoming beautiful.
I look at you.
You are Yann Andréa Steiner.

July 20, Neauphle, afternoon.

Your kisses—I'll believe in them to
the end of my life.
Till we meet again.
Again to no one. Not even to
you.
It's over.

There's nothing.
End the page.
Come now.
We must be going.

Time. Silence, and then.

It must be time for you to do
something. You can't just
do nothing. Maybe you can write.

Silence, and then.

What shall we do in order to live
a little, just a little longer.
No more.
It's no longer me now. It's
someone I no longer know.

Silence, and then.

You can open your heart now. Maybe

I'm the one. I am not lost for you.

Silence, and then.

To make life manageable?
No one knows how. We must try
to live. You can't fling yourself
into death.
No more.
I have no more to say.

July 21.

Come.

I love nothing.

I'll come around you.
Come beside me.
No more.

I want to be protected from that.
Come quick put me somewhere.

Later in the afternoon.

I can't make it any longer.
I don't think this fear can be
given a name. Not yet.

Give me your mouth.
Come quick so we can go quicker.
Quick.
No more.
Quick.

Saturday July 22. Rain.

I'll do nothing more to limit or to enlarge
your life.

Silence.

Come into my face.

Silence.

I'll love you enough not to
abandon you.

Silence.

You are null and void. Nothing.
A double zero.

Sunday July 23.

I cannot bring myself to be nothing.

Silence.

Not being able to be like you
is the sort of thing I regret.

Silence.

Come to bed with me, the big double
bed, and we'll wait.
Nothing.

Silence.

I am frozen by madness.

Y.A.: Do you want to add something?
M.D.: I don't know how to add. All I know how
to do is create. Only that.

Monday July 24.

Come love me.
Come.
Come onto this blank sheet of paper.
With me.

I give you my skin.
Come.
Quick.

Say good-bye to me.
No more.
I know nothing more about you.

I'm going with the sea-weed.
Come with me.

July 31.

What is my own truth?
If you know, tell me.

I am lost.

Look at me.

August 1, afternoon.

It's done, I think. My life
is over.
I am nothing now.
I have become absolutely
frightful.
I no longer hold together.
Come quick.
I have no mouth left, no
face.

Paris, October 12, 1995.

Come into my life.

3:30 in the afternoon.

I am a dead woman. It's over.

Tuesday October 31.

There's no Duras left. I can't take anymore. I have nothing left.

5 in the afternoon.

I am a lover.
You are a lover.

Friday November 3.

Did you ask God to kill me?

Four in the afternoon.

I'd have to have the courage to die.

Thursday November 16.

Beside the sea. Beside you.

I am nothing now. I don't know
where I am. It's over.

Columns to get closer to heaven.
Come.

November 18.

I am a dead woman. It's over.
After this will be hard
for you.

Wednesday November 22.

I am going mad because I have nothing
left. I believe my life is over.
My mouth is tired. There are no more
words.
I have nothing left. No more paper.

December 2.

It's over. I have nothing left.
I have no more mouth, no more face.
Cruel.

Wednesday December 6.

You are an old crow. An old
bastard.

Thursday December 7.

You have a certain strength
in your face.

Friday December 8.

You are all a bunch of idiots.
You're completely fucked up.
It's all unbearable.

Seven in the evening.

Y.A.: What do you feel?
M.D.: The state of death approaching.
It's over. Everything's over. That's
how it is.

December 24.

I don't eat because I have no life left
in me.
Look: my hands are dead.

Tuesday December 26.

I hate psychological pablum.
Disgusting.

Midnight.

There's nothing I want, nothing
packaged. I want a coffee, and right away.

December 27.

Look at me: I'm empty. It's quiet
I need.

December 28.

Stop playing the hero.

December 29.

I have nothing left. I am a dead
woman. I feel it.
Bring me something.

I want to see my mother.

Hurry up.

My whole body is on fire.

Later.

Losing your heart, does that hurt you?

Later.

Come see me, come quick, be with me,
give me something.

Saturday December 30, 2:30 a.m.

You are separated from the realm of Duras.

Wednesday January 3,

The void, or Freedom.

Shut-in women say nothing. They
wait.
A woman alone does not speak.

Saturday, January 6.

Kindness isn't a big deal. What matters
is the extreme thought which leads nowhere,
to nothing.

Later.

Hatred lets you hold on.

January 7.

There's nothing in my head anymore, I
know that.

January 8.

I have nothing left to do but leave.
I don't know where to go.

I've made my fire and everything was white.

I can't find any meaning—and that makes me
alone, not sad, no, alone.

I see black gloves beside me.

Later.

And where does this literature come from?
I like open books.

Come into the white room. Come take off
my white gown. I have nothing left to wear.

It's a splendid life I've made you open.
It has no meaning, but ultimately you believe in it.

I have never forgotten a book.

You are alone for no one. A wretched
misery. A wretched poor woman. Which I am.
And no more.

Don't drop me now, I beg you.
Somewhere deep inside, I am weeping.
Leave me, I am someone free.

Thursday January 18.

My hand is what writes.

January 19.

A confidential pain.

Yann, I should forgive you, I don't know
for what.
I am beautiful. Purely and simply beautiful.

January 25.

This is the end. It is over. This is death.
This is the horror. I hate dying.

I feel a nothing happening: death. And that's frightening.

The eyes are out.
I'm so afraid.
Quick.
I don't believe. I believe I'm completely at sea.

There's nothing. Whatever you do, there's nothing.

I can't write the things that destroy me.

I still love my mother. No help for it, I still
love her.

You can never understand anything, it's a sort of
deficiency. I understand a little.

A sheet of paper, quick. And we're there. And
we
stop. Quick.

Yann, I've loved you so. And now I have to go
away.

I don't know about God every day. You depend
on so little. And afterwards you see. Maybe
every five days?

Friday January 26.

For a few seconds I smelled the fragrance
of earth.

Yann, leave that sacred space, it is frightening.
Sometimes you are frightening.

I've had enough of being alone. I'm going to

hire someone to work on the work.

If I could only do a book on myself and on
what I think. No more. Anything in black
and white.

How hollow you are. And I have always been
in the depths.

January 29.

The void. The void ahead of me.

January 30.

All I know is that I have nothing left.
That is the horror. Nothing left but the
void. The voids. This void of the last
terrain.
There are not two of us. Each of us is alone.

January 31.

Leave me. It's over. Let me die.
I am ashamed.

Friday February 2.

You remember how beautiful. No one since has
been so beautiful as that.

February 15.

The old bedroom where we made love.

February 16.

Odd that I still love you,
even when I don't love you.

Monday, February 19.

I know that I am going to undergo: death.
What awaits me: my face in the morgue.
What a horror, I don't want that.

Later.

All these people wanting the death of
Duras.

Later.

There is not just shame, shame for all of it.
I am nothing now.
Nothing.
I don't know how to exist.
What is not over is the argument of
your person.

Later.

There is the book that wants my death.
Y.A.: Who is the author.

M.D.: Me. Duras.

Tuesday February 20.

Yann, I must ask your forgiveness.
Forgive me for everything.

February 26.

I knew you as someone very strong.
I'm leaving for another latitude.
Nowhere.

February 28.

It's over.
All over.
It is the horror.

Thursday February 29, 1 p.m.

I love you.
Au revoir.

AFTERWORD

Suppose there were a writing of the non-written. Someday
it will come. A brief writing, without grammar, just words. A
writing of words without the support of grammar. Wayward.
Written here. And immediately abandoned.

—MARGUERITE DURAS

There is no paradise in Marguerite Duras. Not even a literary
paradise in which words might find an eternal felicity. She
has not concealed her nostalgia for such a thing. But although
not Edenic, her writing is at least redemptive. Life and literary
invention accommodate themselves miraculously in the
enthusiasm of a nascent inspiration: brief, intense moments of
grace, of inexpressible joys; a door open onto infinity, even onto
immortality.

No More brings Marguerite Duras into confrontation with
the ultimately alien nature of death. Without vanishing, the
perspective constantly deviates. The book gives an impression
of breathlessness, of a visionary spirit exhausted from vertigo,
overwhelmed by a melancholy that diminishes the murmur of
words.

No More echoes a long appeal, ardent and despairing,
stubborn, futile. The world crumbles, the alarming signs of the
end are written everywhere in capital letters.

No More is not a codicil, but a singular testament alternating
meditation and whispered confidences, praise and rage, hope
and regret.

No More, from dedication to farewell, remains a book of love offered to the man whose name appears at the head of the dedication: Yann, the book's other voice.

Thereby, of course, *No More* seems to belie this sentence from *Écrire* (1993): "No one has ever written in two voices," since it presents itself in part as a dialogue in which the author has her—predominant—place, but in which Yann is not separate from the tragedy.

A book in two voices, then? A book which will rouse the curiosity of certain readers? No doubt some will wonder how these scattered fragments have been gathered together, who has bestowed the final touch upon the work. Of course . . . *No More* might be called *The Book of Questions.*

Yet we must attempt to separate the grain from the chaff. At the blind point where words encounter things, far from secondary interrogations, other interrogations appear— primordial ones. Erotic obsession, suffering, the line of fracture between two states of being, lucidity, bewilderment, a now impossible creation, the impossibility of writing, the sentiment of *never more*—this is the labyrinth in which language helplessly tries to beguile death.

A language which insists on being uttered aloud because it exposes at every line the untranslatable nature of life. A violent or helpless language whose secrets must be wrested from it. A language which is inscribed in the ongoing structure of a whole and which does not deter it.

For *No More* exposes old paths. We may approach it outside of its apparent limits. Madness occasionally murmurs here, a conversation with the invisible. The past is remembered. Freed from reassuring chronology, interrupted by silences, it gradually diminishes. By certain expressions we can measure the depth of an imminent and total dispossession of the self which is nonetheless opposed, as if in a kind of exorcism, by a lacerating hymn to life.

How to proceed here—by what itinerary? If it is true that a good reading, according to Marguerite Duras, should start from the "source," following it to the ultimate reservoir of its waters, in order to deliver certain truths, not of the surface but of the depths, permanent truths, no doubt we shall find a necessary premise in the importance of the role played by Yann:

You will have been mine to your very soul.

When Yann comes to Marguerite Duras at Trouville on the Channel coast, in July 1980, though he knows her slightly, though they have exchanged letters, the encounter is now decisive. Fascinated by each other—he by the woman who has written *The Ravishing of Lol Stein* (1964), *India Song* (1973); she by the intelligence and youth of this student of philosophy, by his admiration for her—everything now offers an opportunity to recover the living roots of the erotic passion she has unceasingly celebrated in her life and in her books.

That abominably stable summer, she seems abandoned by Venus, who had so often rewarded her. Many recent works proclaim her abandonment, which nonetheless finds no ally in *la délectation morose*. Work now resumes, for the absent hour, the task of love. Always richly confident in life, Marguerite Duras transforms the void into expectation. Rebellious, she sends up her distress signals; as in *Le Navire Night* (1979): "And then nothing more happened. Nothing more. Nothing. Except always, everywhere, those cries, that same lack of love." And in *The Truck* (1977): "She might have said straight off: there is no story outside of love." Or again, in *Les Mains Négatives* (1979): "I summon the one who will answer me. I want to love you I love you." Belatedly, *Writing* explains the suffering of those years and the help afforded by work: "To find yourself in a hole, at the bottom of a hole, in a virtually total solitude and to discover that only writing will save you."

The summer of 1980 inaugurates a fruitful renewal and institutes an erotic future of which she had reported, in 1977, to her friend Michèle Manceaux: "When one has heard the body—I should say desire, whatever is imperious in oneself . . . if one has not known the passion which takes this form, physical passion, one knows nothing."

Three years later, Yann knocks at her door while she remains silent, moved: "ten years ago I was living in a very strict, almost cloisteral solitude." At grips with a new ardor, wrenched from her soliloquies, she turns from isolation to ecstasy. *No More* reflects that fire which prowls on the confines of words and assures the text's irreplaceable particularity. Throughout, memories glisten, the determination to withstand disappointments or failures provokes love-cries with complex echoes. And these cries, as much as the desperate fever to keep death at a distance, as much as the despairing shame of being unable to hold onto life, inscribe the book's lines of force. Lines of flight as well, for erotic discourse involves an endless wandering in the forest of signs, disperses in enigmatic impressions, and is lost in the depths of consciousness.

Her body a captive of every one of her senses, extenuated by reason of her weakness and illness, caught in the trap of her eyes fixed on the lover of the night, frequently clairvoyant about herself, Marguerite Duras manages to produce the words which release her and commemorate the transports of this passionate adventure. Whereby we recognize her readily enough. Nothing deletes the fundamental power which she confers upon love: "The word love exists," she maintains on June 28, 1995.

Nonetheless, we observe on the one hand that if this word persists down to the last lines of *No More,* it yields to the death which haunts this universe and which is ever more chaotic, ratified, abysmal. As in her books? Yes, except that the stake here is of a different nature. Two antithetical absolutes do battle in an unequal combat won in advance, lost in advance. Forever.

On the other hand, following her natural tendency, if Marguerite Duras clearly designates Yann as the object of her love, she does not avoid certain intervals which frustrate the biographical, projecting it into the vagueness of a tutelary dream. Incontestably, desire for Yann is expressed in terms of the woman who experiences it. Homage rendered to its charm is not lacking:

You are becoming beautiful.
I look at you.

Desire mobilizes attention, sensitive to this or that aspect of the lover, to his hands which *advance with the hill,* to his blondness, to his strength. Sometimes the fear of a distraction is apparent: "I have not said enough about his person, his soul, his feet, his hands, his laughter." We shall not be surprised to find such terms indissociably yoked together. Soul and hands, feet and laughter, all are of equal worth for Marguerite Duras. Hence the effusion, of a carnal order, which she can whisper to herself, in a delicate incantation, a tender lullaby:

I wait for you the way I wait for

someone who will destroy this failed
grace, gentle and still warm.
Given to you, wholly, with my
whole body, this grace.

Or, without any evasion, quite directly:

Give me your mouth.
Come quick so we can go quicker.
Quick.
No more.
Quick.

Such subjugation, which is also a feature of possessiveness with
regard to Yann, does not escape thought's slippage toward ill-
defined, unidentifiable characters, a dream procession, other
faces of love.

I want to talk about someone.
About a man of twenty-five
at the most.
He is a beautiful man . .

Or:

The name: I don't know.
It is not important.
To be together as with a
lover.
I would have liked that to happen to me.

With *No More,* Marguerite Duras has entered a region unknown to her where all points of reference are turned upside down. On July 24, 1995, she feels herself to be frozen by madness. On December 29, her whole body is in flames. Nonetheless, the love sought for, hoped for, found at last, lost, regained, has never broken out of the circle in which it has remained since her first affair. Sometimes it appers to escape this circle in order to focus on a lover, on someone. But the escape does not seem indispensable, for love does not manifest itself only by the impulse toward the other. As we read in *Emily L.* (1987), love closes over itself, mutates into a way of being:

> I wanted to tell you what I believe. Which is that you
> must always keep for yourself, yes, that is the word for
> it, a place, a sort of personal place, that's right, to be
> alone there and to love. To love you don't know what,
> nor whom nor how, nor for how long. To love, and
> now suddenly all the words are coming back to me . . .
> to keep inside yourself the place to await such a love,
> perhaps a love without a person as yet, but for that and
> that alone, for love.

If the lover erases contingency, if he remains a chosen intermediary by which the world recovers its lustre, he is not, for all that, the subject of a cult offered to him alone. He may serve as the excuse for an apology of desire for desire's sake, having no hold over the woman who loves him. She will never release her prey for some illusion—that is, will never surrender her autonomy, for the sake of fidelity to the lover, however seductive. On occasion the lover may be alarmed or irritated:

What you wanted was this contradiction: to be in a
love which fulfilled you and to summon another love
to the rescue.

To which the retort is made, still in *Emily L:* "Not entirely . . .
neither to summon another love nor even to hope for such a
thing. Only to write within it, to write out of it."

To write, to love. Both lead to disorders and to delights, both
are experienced in the same defiance of knowledge reduced to
despair, both come to terms with the most opaque realms of the
mind where nothing is mastered. Consequently, anatagonistic
impulses follow each other or interlace. Sometimes Marguerite
Duras is interested in the individual relation which the lover
sustains with the beloved, the writer with her book. Sometimes,
on the contrary, she imagines a circulation of desire and of
the work, an infinite and utopian extension which exceeds all
jealousy. *Destroy, She Said* (1969) illustrates this with regard to
love, and in *Woman to Woman: Les Parleuses* (1974) she rejoices
that the writing emerges from its sacred sheath to circulate as
well. Does one borrow chapters? Does an author appropriate
them with a view to inserting them into her personal
publications? Why not:

That I myself should have written it matters much less
than the accuracy of what is written.

Concerned with this charaacter of the work, she readily
acknowledges a community, a new country without borders,
that of writing: "When we write, when we call, already we are
alike," affirms *Le Navire Night:*

'You' is sometimes 'I'.
I say 'I' and I am not 'I'.
'I' is you, and you are going to die.

To write. To write short anxious notes. To write what is passing through your head or your body. To write in the chaos before there were any words, before the inadmissable: "I can't write anymore." Before the moment when the spoken will be the improbable substitute of the written, though preserving a tonality comparable to no other, already proceeding from elsewhere, though seeking a meagre consolation: "Writing is very close to the rhythm of speech," for as we realize, proximity does not signify identity.

When he is close to her, a man takes the time to listen, to share this confidential suffering: Yann, discreet to the point of self-effacement or suddenly pressing her with questions, as always an indefatigable secretary. Marguerite Duras explains the meaning of their reciprocal attachment: "Being together is love, death, speaking, sleeping." A phrase corroborated by *Summer 80* and *Practicalities: Duras Speaks to Jérôme Beaujour* (1987) among other books which illuminate a tormented alliance, punctuated by smiles and ordeals, a passion filled with tumult, between living and dying. Of which the fictions—that lying-as-truth, according to the poet Aragon's formula—evoke the long shadows, the bare spaces, and the magical current which traverses them.

After *Summer 80,* Yann penetrates to the heart of her literary creation and is indissolubly associated with it until 1996. Marguerite Duras maintains that if at the period of *Aurélia Steiner* (1979) she addresses him, it is so that he may obtain a preferred place between Aurélia and herself, having actually been the cause of that work. Later, she offers him a jumble of texts which she has already published in newspapers or magazines, to which are added prefaces and interviews. He organizes them and writes a long explanatory note which follows the preface. In 1981 the book appears signed by Marguerite Duras under the title *Outside*. Henceforth Yann becomes sometimes the dedicatee, sometimes the hero, as in *No More,* the interlocutor and always the lover, always a presence in the site which is the page, a white surface blackened with lines, in the actual volume of her books. A site of variable geometry, a verbal space sometimes encumbered by reality. Nor is Marguerite Duras at all blind to the nature of that reality. From the first she apprehends the precariousness of such a love: the difference in age between herself and Yann—she is 66, he is not yet 29—seems insignificant when set beside his homosexuality, perceived as an even greater obstacle.

In the course of the articles she writes for *Libération,* from the end of June 1980, collecting and publishing them in September under the title *Summer 80,* she describes certain political or social events, what might be called: news. An occasional journalist, she doubles the public chronicle with a private one. Pondering the rebellion of the Polish miners in Gdansk, their repression and Moscow's attitude, she finds nothing more pessimistic except, she adds, "this love of mine for you, which I know is illusory and which my apparent preference for you proves that I love only love itself, not dismantled by the choice of our history." Dismantled or not, however, love persists and endures and engenders many texts, several of which are cited in *No More.* Others appear there implicitly.

On November 28, 1994, there is a discussion of *The Malady of Death* (1982):

I must speak of the man in *The Malady of Death*.
Who is he?
How did he come to be here?
Write about his thin build,
write starting from the man's thin build.

Time has no deleterious effect on memory. At least in this place. Nor on the harsh will to understand. Nor on the inquisitorial function which is understandable if we recall this dialogue from *The Malady of Death*, if we note the bitter irony of the final remark:

She asks: "Have you never desired a woman?" You say, "No, never."
She asks: "Not even once? Not even for a moment?" You say, "No, never."
She says: "Never?" You repeat, "Never."
She smiles. She says: "A dead man is a strange thing."

Against the impossibility of a persistent passion, bearing within it an incurable wound, writing is, from the first, a defence. That love should be jeopardized from the very start, that it must constantly be reinvented, involves a certain distress though one that literature feeds on. It produces a strange fusion between lover and beloved. As July 3, 1995, proves:

You are in the strongest spell
I have ever seen.
You are responsible for everything.
Whatever I've done you could have done.

Previously there appears an allusion to *The Atlantic Man* (1981, the film 1982). Yann's departure, a definitive escape which will be no such thing, has justified the publication of this book and the making of the film, at the heart of which there is no concealment of affliction: "I have said aloud the date of the day it was, Monday, June 15, 1981, when you left forever in that terrible heat and I believed, yes, that time I believed it was forever." It is hardly necessary to repeat that in its Latin origins the word "passion" reveals those links which unite it to suffering. One of the worst agonies, for Marguerite Duras, was the failure of desire, fading or vanishing; to narrate such disenchantment, to confess it, establishes a protective distance. The world of words safeguards the real world, or enables her to endure it. Yann gone, these are the thoughts which overwhelm the narrator:

> I no longer love you the way I did the first day. I no longer love you. There remain, however, around your eyes, those places which surround your gaze, and that existence which animates you in your sleep.
>
> There also remains that exaltation which comes to me from no longer knowing what to make of all this—of that knowledge I have of your eyes, of the immensities your eyes explore—so that I no longer know what to write.

The determination not to tolerate this state of affairs reappears:

> While I no longer love you, I love nothing,
> nothing but you even so.

Close, in many regards, to a phrase in *No More* of February 16, 1996:

> Odd that I still love you,
> even when I don't love you.

Amid these apparent contradictions, nothing obliterates the book's design. An additional proof that the book relegates the experience of pain to oblivion merely by recomposing it in the powerful web of language. If writing refers to life, much more often life refers to writing. Hence we must pay close attention to the notice sent to the press upon the publication of *Blue Eyes, Black Hair* (1986):

> This is the story of a love, the greatest and most
> terrifying I have had to write. I know that One
> knows such things for oneself. It is the story of a love
> not named in novels and not named by those who
> experience it. It is the story of a lost love. Lost, as in
> perdition.

No transition between narration and the experience. The true and the false, the real and the imaginary, are inextricably mingled. This, on account of the mental structure of an author who, throughout her existence, cultivates her gifts for the art of transposition, so that in the last resort the text alone holds the truth and tolerates no contestation, as we discern in this other commentary on *Blue Eyes, Black Hair*:

> What I want to tell here is a love story which is still
> possible even when it presents itself as impossible to

the eyes of people who are far from writing—writing not being concerned by whether or not the story is possible.

The last remark applies to the entirety of the work, but assumes a stronger resonance after the 1980s. It also illuminates this prayer to Yann of July 24, 1995, in *No More:*

> Come love me.
> Come.
> Come onto this blank sheet of paper.
> With me.

Blank sheet of paper, white page, the erotic event becomes an event of writing. In other words, love and language are constitutive of one another, and their analogies incite the reader never to separate memory and imagination. Life is not art. Art is not obliged to respect a literal reality. Its duties are only to itself.

In 1982 Yann publishes a book entitled *M.D.,* the story of a young man keeping a journal of a disintoxication cure—that of the heroine of this book, M.D. With her he used to drink to excess. He does not leave her when she is hospitalized. At her bedside he writes down what he observes, what he hears, what he feels: hallucinations, doctors' advice, his fears and his hopes. When M.D. recovers, the testimony comes to an end with these words: "I write to keep you close to me, to diminish the separation, to bind you to mortality." A pledge of love, absolute faith in the power of language and demonstration of a complicity acknowledged by both parties.

For Yann collaborates in Marguerite Duras's work. He types

her manuscripts from dictation two hours a day. He also takes her for automobile rides in the Normandy countryside or around Paris and accompanies her on her travels. Sometimes quarrels break out. He loses his temper, shouts, leaves, returns at five in the morning. In 1986, here is what *The Slut of the Normandy Coast* learns: "I didn't tell him I couldn't write because of his cries and because of what I regarded as his unfairness toward me. Soon, even when he was away, I couldn't write." One might say that Marguerite Duras wants Yann to be an equal, an autonomous writer, even with her help. It is this stormy but lasting complicity which is responsible for the birth of *No More*. Marguerite Duras underlines the fact on the afternoon of July 3, 1995:

> Everything was written by you, by that
> body you have.
> I'm going to stop this text here and
> go on with another by you, made for
> you, made instead of you.

But she cannot elude the flow of time. Words fail her now, inexorably devoured by the void, a leit-motif in the text. This terror corrupts any effusion, mutilates her will, and destroys the likelihood of even the slightest task. Every attempt at lucidity gives way to the sentiment of chaos. Thought disintegrates and soon borders on unreason. Thus the breach is widened between the woman who will die and the man who will survive:

> You are here, but this place is so huge that to be close
> together means being already so far apart that we
> manage neither to see nor to hear one another.

Who knows if others besides Marguerite Duras would consent to the oblique light of death which falls across the rooms where she writes, where she speaks, in Paris, Rue Saint-Benoît, in Neauphle-le-Château, in her beloved house. Some might domesticate—if not welcome it with such lofty impassivity. Still others might turn away, might sink to the bottom of the night, paralyzed, mute.

Loyal to herself, Marguerite Duras pays tribute to the funereal festival of *No More*. For her, everything requires a transition to the word, to the accent of the voice. How else, aspiring as she does only to life, could she consent to that slow labor of decomposition in the obscurity of the body, in the meanders of the mind? Frequently a lucid desolation brings her to a halt confronting her fallen countenance, her irremediable isolation, the fear of her dislocated identity. So many demons swarm around her, wrenching her from the profusion of her past existence:

I have a meager life now.
Poor.
I have become poor.

The intuition of decrepitude:

I have no more mouth, no more face.
Cruel.

Undisguised terror:

What awaits me: my face in the morgue.
What a horror, I don't want that.

And a hundred incommunicable impressions:

> It's done, I think. My life
> is over.
> I am nothing now.
> I have become absolutely
> frightful.

Except at the very end of the book, where horror, pleas for forgiveness, and farewells seem to derive from certain ancestral rituals because the death sentence, if it severs her from the world of the living, delivers in return the possibility of uttering what are called: the last words. *No More* makes no sacrifice to tradition and refuses to be mastered by compromise. Quite the contrary, it defies death by the intense impulses of desire, the rich texture of the phrases Marguerite Duras creates by a sudden denial of physical and moral attrition, by a furious abruptness, by perpetual oscillations from one pole to the other, secret energies that are primitive, elementary, radical. In doing so, the writer traces the capricious trajectory of her works, especially after 1980.

Elusive, polymorphous, protean, her passion for Yann is the brightest thread in a tightly woven texture.

> Before and now it is love between us,
> between you and me.
> Death and love.

And if love, as we are well aware, has always marked Marguerite Duras for its own, with Yann it extends its empire farther than she dared hope. A fire born from the ashes, it is from its lack of satisfaction, from its torments that it derives all its wonders and, better still, its longevity. This was apparent as early as *Agatha* (1981)—a fictional variant—in which the incest taboo between brother and sister is doubled by a separation insisted upon by the latter, not at all out of a concern for morality but with a view to perpetuating passion. Agatha, the heroine, believes that the taboo will then be more redoutable, more terrifying, unknown, accursed, senseless, intolerable, as close as possible to the intolerable, as close as possible to this love.

In *No More* love has not faded. It murmurs its existence, proclaims itself, sings out. Occasionally, with the sweetness of a plaint

Yann.
I hope to see you at the end of the afternoon.
With all my heart.
With all my heart.

Occasionally in the form of a direct and emphatic invitation:

COME
Come with me.
Quick, come.

Occasionally by means of peremptory assertions:

Love too great between us,
even to horror.

Or:

You are what you are, and that
delights me.

Or:

That you love me is the most important thing.
The rest doesn't matter to me. The hell
with it.

To all this, no answers. At least, the text indicates none. On the other hand, it tends toward a link with a constant of Marguerite Duras's temperament: her inclination toward rebellion. Crushed by living, overwhelmed, lost, she says on January 6, 1966: "Hate: that helps you hold on." Holding on, that is the key word. Less than anyone in the world can she resign herself to being nothing. By what means is she to struggle against ruin? Nothing is to be overlooked in her wild attempt to triumph over fate. If the incantation of language is insufficient, she reassures herself by manifest truths: "Yann, I am still here" or "I am upset that the decades pass by so fast. But I am still on this side of the world." For a long time her stubbornness is unrelenting, and her bravery. She compels herself to track down the life which evades and so cruelly transforms her: "I love life, even the way it is here . . . You must try to live. You cannot fling yourself into death." Elsewhere a way of eluding nothingness, she throws herself into everyday, prosaic trifles: food, drink, money:

Tonight we'll have something very strong
to eat. Something Chinese, for instance . . .

I want a coffee, and right away . . .

You don't have to worry about
the money.

In 1987 *Practicalities* brimmed over with such details, those of a woman whose place is defined by her domesticity, a role that remains unchanged, according to this writer, despite the evolution of *mores*. The recurrence of the quotidian in *No More* can only confirm the fact.

Other horizons appear, which refer to *Emily L.,* in which the narrator discusses death with a blond young man. They joke about it together. Suddenly, having declared that no one can endure death, she adds, for his sake: "But for you, this is nothing. Put yourself in my place." The standard formula, here located in a playful context, sounds quite different when set beside certain passages of *No More.* To put himself in her place is what Yann cannot do. And his own life opens an impassable gulf between Marguerite Duras and himself. The woman who so proudly wrote in *Les Yeux verts* (1980): "When I write I do not die. Who would die when I write?" reaches the dreaded conclusion. She no longer writes. She dies. Alone. Anticipation of her imminent disappearance provokes not lamentation but rage, a sort of tragic fury against the ones—and especially the one—not there. Against those who have shown no concern, who are ignorant of the state of death, such rage is revealed here in a swipe of her talons: "Yann, don't you feel you're a kind of dependency of Duras?"; there in a prophecy of worse to come: "You head straight for solitude. Not me, I have books."; and later still, with an aggressive humor: "It must be time for you to do something. You can't just do nothing." or else, by the wounding and wounded lie: "I think of no one. The rest is over. You as well."

And gradually the tone intensifies: "You are null and void. Nothing. A double zero." "You are an old crow. An old bastard." The whole world is in her sights: "You are all a bunch of idiots. You're completely fucked up. It's all unbearable." Which suggests a sentence from The Truck: "Let the world go down to destruction," with a certain dramatic exaggeration. Beyond these insults or the curse which is accounted for by the insurmountable despair of loneliness, of destruction, impotence, exhaustion in the face of the lover's vital forces, appears the essential regret: "Not to be able to be like you," following the limpid confession: "I cannot bear your future." Everything happens as if, sustained by her fictions to the very end, she vaguely wants Yann to join her in the grave where death will seal their love forever. "I'm going down with the weeds. Come with me." Excess typical of the writer, a queen dispossessed of the kingdom from which she banishes her lover because he fails to join her in another kingdom, that of the shades.

Amid all this exasperation can be heard a wish which will not be granted, the wish that Marguerite Duras attributed in 1960 to a character in *Hiroshima mon amour:* "I'd like to stay with you." *No More* extends this wish in a grave, infinitely distressed form: "Yann, I've loved you so. And now I have to go away." By what premonition did she write in *The Ravishing of Lol Stein:* "I deny the end which will probably come to separate us, I deny its ease, its dreadful simplicity, for from the moment that I deny it, I accept the other ending, the one which is still to be invented, which I don't know, which no one has invented yet"?

All these vicissitudes, the tidal movements which are to be perceived in the book, come to an end by dissolving into each other, into one and the same affective coloration. On the brink of the fatal date, as in *Summer 80,* Yann is compared to a child. He has given birth to "a love without direction which had the fragrance of the flesh of a child dying to read the enigma of desire." He has restored the writer to the iridescent reflexions of her own remote childhood, furnishing memories which circle round her, like a dance.

Where are you going?
Toward the well of my childhood, and following
death's path.

Each of Marguerite Duras's texts, if it occupies a specific position, can be properly understood only in relation to her other texts. Few bodies of work are so homogeneous as hers, possess so visible a geography, where the rivers invert their course, the sea its tides, where the landscapes, the characters, the circumstances all recall, in a more or less masked fashion, those of the Cochin China of her birth. What matters is to return to the source. What source, or rather sources?

Most of Marguerite Duras's writings refer to her early youth and often derive from that period. *No More* does not abrogate this law. Here the writer freely establishes certain details, as they present themselves, quite without affectation. Thus she continues to be the persevering archeologist of her own history. If Yann asks her which of her books she prefers to all the others, the answer bursts out: *"The Sea Wall,* childhood."

At the heart of this childhood, the mother, origin within origin, an ambiguous figure if we are to credit *The Lover* (1984): "filth, my mother, my love." The mother, one of the capital characters, the one that is not forgotten despite her injustice, despite her preference for her sons, despite her incomprehensions. Here nothing counts any longer except this woman, purged of her failings, in a memory where love wins out over hatred:

> I still love my mother. No help for it, I still
> love her.

As though summoned from beyond, Marguerite Duras utters a child's cry: "I want to see my mother," and in terror, she joins her:

> The fear is less solid.
> Leave me here where I am with
> my mother's fear of death, remaining
> intact, whole.

The mother, love, death sustain close affinities. Paired by necessity and the nature of things, they superimpose, by a girational movement, every beginning and every end. Symbol of the eternal return, they strew the texts of Marguerite Duras, determining their meaning and their form. Emblematic metaphor of a structure of repetition, for, as stated, each book is born from the one which, more or less remotely, precedes it and links it, more or less rigorously, to the one which follows. *The Lover* or *The North China Lover* (1991) resume *The Sea Wall* (1950), several situations of which already figure in *Les Impudents* (1943) or *La Vie tranquille* (1944). *The Ravishing of Lol Stein, The Vice-Consul* (1965), *L'Amour* (1971) or the film *India Song* (1975), itself adapted from the text of 1973, which preludes another film, *Son nom de Venise dans Calcutta désert* (1976), find the same characters reappearing in a different light, linked by an altered set of calculations. These examples suffice. Until *No More,* every text anticipates another. All end by interlacing. An arabesque, one might say, if it were a matter of sculpture or drawing, a fugue in music, in any case a schema which exfoliates around a radiating center. An inexhaustible task of analogy, by countless combinations, separate volutes which a single principle coordinates, without a gap but by an incessant transition from the other to one and from one to the other, the writing evolves.

Tirelessly Marguerite Duras inventories "the most extraordinary moments of life," which is to say, childhood, as *Emily L.* suggests. If she turns away from them, she is deceived and overcome by regret. Self-criticism reveals the allegiance to the times and places of childhood:

> As each time these memories came back to me,
> they distanced me from you all, in the same way as
> a memory of some reading for which I could not be
> comforted, the reading of that part of my own writings
> which concerned a certain period of my youth, and
> I was thinking that I had to leave you to write some
> more about Siam and about other things which none
> of you had known, and that I kept having to go back
> to Siam especially, that sky above the mountain and
> those other things I had thought of then that I should
> have passed over in silence and about which now,
> quite the opposite, I believed I should have clung to all
> my life.

Behind Asia stretches a mysterious continent, still Asia but an Asia in which lived, according to *The Lover,* a family of white hooligans and a Chinese lover. An Asia revisited. It belongs to the writer alone. No intruder is admitted there. In a theater, are not the wings concealed from the audience? And if, perhaps, some inquisitive person manages to sneak in, is he not chased away? A similar rule guides Marguerite Duras as soon as someone approaches that patch of ground within her sights.

One of her biographers believes she has disgraced herself by daring to retrace a life which no documentation or archive, no journey to Saigon, no photograph can ever restore as her works succeed in doing. When Marguerite Duras granted the rights of *The Lover* to the film-maker Jean-Jacques Annaud who shot the film in 1991, she immediately produced a huge fresco called *The North China Lover,* of which the preface indicates: "This book might have been called *The Lover Begun Again.*" And later we read: "In the cinema there is a choice. Either we remain on the mother's face as she describes without seeing. Or we see the table and the children described by the mother. The author prefers this second proposition." All these remarks become scathing and suggest the substance of endless polemics, if we fail to regard them principally as the irresistible attraction of a reconquest.

Even if, as the guardian of her memories, Marguerite Duras insists on retaining their exclusive rights and refuses to grant them to others, the profound reasons for such intransigence are not explained merely by the sentiment of an eviction. For her, the precise historical event, verifiable or painstakingly reconstituted, has neither weight nor value in itself. Weight and value come from the imaginary charge she attributes to it. She is delivered from the reality of which, at her discretion, she modifies the reminiscence in order to subordinate it to language. Why? Because there is no equivalence between reality and language. In a writer's eyes, the words are worth more than the facts. If they seem to refute the facts, it is to bring them into a more violent, more probing light. Differently oriented, they gain a mythological dimension. Their least arguable mission consists, then, in eclipsing the usual for the sake of a new organization, one that will be free and autonomous, by which the author returns to her constrained territory, unconcerned by contradictions, as often as she desires—returns, here, to childhood, that port, that sheltered harbor, auroral point of all departures:

> Through you I go back to the origin of the sign, to the free writing sketched by the wind on the sea and the sand, to the wild writing of the birds.

From one origin to the other. The second is more complex. It does not concern the source of inspiration, but inspiration itself, the reflex of time which separates the writer from the world in order to restore her to it after an incomparable experience which Marguerite Duras has baptized *the marvellous misfortune:*

> The writings which seem most finished are
> merely aspects quite remote from what has been
> glimpsed, that inaccessible tonality which escapes
> all understanding (. . .) The marvellous misfortune
> is perhaps just such torment, that solicitation which
> permits no respite, that uprooting of the self which
> leaves you lost and abandoned.

Contrary to several of her contemporaries, Nathalie Sarraute, Michel Butor, and Alain Robbe-Grillet, Marguerite Duras published no theoretical work on the novel. Empirical, in the sense that she receives nothing as true of which she has not herself apprehended the cause or the basis, she postulates a knowledge not susceptible of demonstration, entirely personal: "I always speak about myself, you know. I speak of what I know." And indeed, far from any doctrine, she wades into the dense and nebulous universe of her creation in pursuit of the meaning of the writing which constantly escapes and nonetheless legitimizes her attempts.

In this experience, what most demands her attention is the initial moment, the first gesture toward the white sheet on which she sets down the rough drafts, the first attempt to render them legible by others without their losing their raw power. Hence she annexes the material act of writing to her books: "My hand is what writes," she says in *No More,* and elsewhere: "I still feel the effort of my hand to write quickly, not to forget." For her major concern is the literal transcription of what has invaded her—voice, images—even before she organizes it, before it must be reduced, unified, arranged. A quarrel of the self with itself in *Practicalities:* "How to speak of it, how to describe what I knew and what was there, in the quasi-tragic refusal to pass into writing, as if it were impossible." A provisional solution of the problem in *Emily L:* "To fling the writing out, to mistreat it almost, yes, to mistreat it, to take nothing away from its useless mass, nothing, to leave it whole with the rest, to correct nothing, neither speed nor slowness, to leave everything in the state of its first appearance."

The resemblance is exact between the compost of childhood and the childhood of writing. In both prevails a savage disobedience and unruliness, fervor, impulsiveness, pleasure and terrors. The text confirms this:

Writing makes you wild. You link up with a primordial wildness. And you always recognize it, it is the wildness of the woods, as old as time. The wildness of total fear, distinct and inseparable from life itself. You are in a frenzy. You cannot write without the body's strength. You have to be stronger than yourself to contend with writing, you have to be stronger than what you are writing. It's a funny thing, yes. It's not only writing, what you write, it's the cries of animals in the night, and of everything else, of you and me, of the dogs. It's the massive, heartbreaking vulgarity of society. Suffering is Christ too and Moses and the pharaohs and all the Jews, and all the Jewish children, and also the most violent kind of happiness. That's what I've always believed . . . When I write, I participate in the same madness as in life. I join the masses of stone when I write. The stones of the Sea Wall.

Madness, savagery, primordial power of language—it is hard to imagine how these distinctive features of Marguerite Duras's writing could be caught in the nets of a classical construction, could be inserted into the pure line of time in which the successive moments peacefully cohabit. Her time is always out of synch, behind or ahead of itself. And as her oeuvre extends, the narratives become more capricious. In 1980, *Les Yeux verts* expresses what has already become a necessity and will not cease being so for the writer—an esthetic of discontinuity: "I am compelled to proceed by an apparent fragmentation of the writing, of the tenses which structure it, and above all to keep changing the direction of its components." It is in this way that the sentence achieves an organic dimension. It espouses the profusion of the world, welcomes its chaos, renders its infinite diversity, and progresses, expressive to a fault, by its repetitions and its strophic forms.

Nonetheless, in *No More,* the writer is in exile from herself: "It's no longer me now. It's someone I no longer know." This new condition puts her in jeopardy: "I no longer have the slightest notion about what I thought I knew," she concedes, and: 'The rest, before, after me, ahead and behind me, is a matter of indifference." We feel that Marguerite Duras would prefer to stop time, to establish herself at the heart of a motionless present in which she would employ, once and for all, all the words. As it is, this present-tense floods her and becomes blurred, wavers in painful anticipation and assumes an hallucinatory unreality:

> There is no present tense. There is a past haunted by the future and a future drawn and quartered by the present.

Just as, in *No More,* her body seems to be cut into pieces—"I no longer hold together"—so too the discourse is strewn with lacunae, and the temporality wavers in an imprecise oscillation. The book distributes the moments according to obscure imperatives, bringing provisional motifs into play, setting them aside and then re-examining them. Appearance, disappearance, speculations as to the future, descents into an unspecifiable past, close or remote, the prevailing impression, at first glance, is that of a chaotic scattering. As if one were contemplating a dust of islands—an archipelago.

Dated November 20, 1994, the first fragment and those which follow afford no offence to linearity until around the 28th of the same month. Then, back to October 14 then a leap ahead to December 10. The year is ending. Nothing clearly indicates that we are approaching 1995. And, if April 9 corresponds to Palm Sunday, this appears, in the text, only after Good Friday and Holy Saturday, that is, April 14 and 15. But Easter is not mentioned on the 16, and the text moves on to the 19. Then to the end of spring and the beginning of summer. From January 3 to February 29 1996, as at the beginning of the book, chronology is respected once again.

Why this confusion? The possibility cannot be eliminated that Yann has collected the scattered pieces of the writing, that he has chosen to intervene or not to intervene in this drifting text. But from the start one voice catches our attention, as if we were not reading, rather as if we were listening to that series of words all the more attentively because the woman who is uttering them indicates an extreme weariness. Moreover, Marguerite Duras has always shown a preference not for an inexorable clock time, but to the more disturbing, unexpected, fruitful time of memory. *The Lover,* among so many other books, does not proceed from past to present without shocks. It confuses the periods without any more transition than a dotted line. The shadow of the veranda where, around 1925, the children watch the mountain of Siam is not set apart from the death of the younger brother in 1942. Nor the girlfriends of wartime, Marie-Claude Carpenter or Betty Fernandez, from the little white girl returning repeatedly to the State Institution, accompanied in the limousine by the Chinaman from Cholen.

No More perpetuates the process and increases its importance. Perhaps, here, this wandering, this way of taking short-cuts, amount to a sentimental means of avoiding the road which leads straight from the cradle to the grave. Perhaps the fragmentation suggests the omnipresence of the threat of death which eats away at the book. The threshhold sentence links the uncertainty of the day—"You never know"—to anteriority—"before"—to impatience—"hurry up." Duration vanishes. The text establishes only the absurd and fugitive aspect of the present moment which is parcelled out between the destroyed past and the destructive future. Assailed from both sides, it vanishes, sometimes dissolved in the tide of memories, sometimes reduced to the idea of death, to the unthinkable. The final combat of Eros and Thanatos. From this point of view, the book might be recapitulated like this:

I wanted to tell you
that I loved you.
To shout it.
No more.

Many sentences or paragraphs reveal a predilection for the period which saw her united to Yann, a period precious because it has illuminated a life that must soon be abandoned. "You remember how beautiful. No one since has been so beautiful as that." she said on February 2, 1966. On the 15, these few words— "The old bedroom where we made love."—substantiate Marcel Proust: the memory of a certain image is merely the regret for a certain moment. Idealization of a space which is, somewhat differently, discussed in *Summer SO.* The more abundant expression was nuanced there: "This room might have been the place where we would have made love, this is the place, then, of our love." If the past conditional makes the passion uncertain, the present comes to the rescue and imposes conviction. In *Emily L.* the lover protected himself and the narrator attributed these words to him:

You have invented for me. I count for nothing in the
story you have had with me.

And she herself retorted:

You said the opposite, once, at the beginning.

In *No More*, the time is no longer under discussion. Thought
is attached to the still intense emotion, to the "The beginning
of the end of that really terrifying love, with the regret for each
hour," and drifts:

And then there was the hour that followed,
incomprehensible, emerging from the depths
of time.
Horrible hour.
Splendid and horrible.

What hour was that? *Yann Andréa Steiner: A Memoir* (1992)
affords an answer. After the night of love he describes,
Marguerite Duras conceives a violent need to utter an "I love
you," but she is alone under the noon sky, a sky of wind and
rain. She is convinced that Yann does not know why he has
come to Trouville, to her house, the house of an old woman,
mad from writing. The notion pursues her, the unexpected sign
of a terrible perplexity.

And *No More* continues. Partly anarchic, releasing, in the
looseness of conversation, an unendurable terror, a low and
continuous note that vibrates beneath each word. On March
25, 1995, it comes forth: "It is so hard to die." A few months
afterwards, as in Monteverdi's madrigal Lasciatemi morire, a

plea makes itself heard: "Leave me... Let me die." After July 28, repeating of the words: end, finished, over, lost, nothing, empty, forms a grim litany, almost without tears, stripped of all rhetorical effect, pure acknowledgement of the inevitable descent into the abyss.

That a human being's birth dooms that being to death is a truth impossible to accept. Not knowing either when or how death will come, one postulates that it is not for tomorrow. The future is so vague that certainty dissolves. Suddenly one day, one is brought face to face with death. One is overwhelmed by the event, at once so foreseeable and so unexpected. A paralyzed spectator, Marguerite Duras is present at this drama and it is she herself who is on stage, helpless victim of a stupefied dread. The bird that enters her bedroom and flies out, at the end of 1994—is it not just like the one her mother said she saw, in *The Lover,* just before her husband's disappearance? Is it not the harbinger of death, the messenger of disaster?

In this confusion, at moments, visions overwhelm her which the Surrealists would not have disavowed, so faint now is the control of reason. The blind eyes next to a pair of black gloves seem to have emerged from a Luis Bunuel film, that self-portrait: "I am a stick of wood" from a poem by André Breton, and the strangeness of the universe rendered colorless by the fire, from a picture by Max Ernst.

Against all common measurement, this sudden whiteness acts like the cloak of night. It effects a negation of space, an erasure of her perception, and a negation of time in which irreconcilable oppositions appear: beauty proudly insisted on and a dreadful countenance, disdainful dismissal and humble prayer, dependance and a stubborn affirmation of freedom.

Between the self tending towards its own annihilation and

defined now only by withdrawal, nothingness on the one hand, and on the other its immediate surroundings, the distance grows still greater. In November 1994 there is a question of a summer afternoon like this one, and on the 22nd, in the Paris apartment, the writer speaks of her arrival at the seaside. October 14, 1994, seems to coincide with October 14, 1914. By what association of ideas? The text closes over the inexplicable. The words seem to have no other function than to occupy a time and a space without connections. Defeated, Marguerite Duras does not differ from her defeated language on the white page:

> In this book, he was saying, the writing is absence and the white page presence. Thus God who is absence is present in the book.

Down through the years, Marguerite Duras treats language with a great economy of means. Aside from the very first books, a great deal is made of silence and blank space. As for this latter, the typographical arrangements are not accidental. These remarkable procedures confer upon the texts one of their stylistic features. They are based on the notion of lack, of void, of the unspeakable.

In *Moderato Cantabile* (1958), how many unfinished sentences, how many points of suspension, and how many spaces between Yann Andréa Steiner's lines in 1992? The reader is confronted with a perforated text, where the black of the writing plays with the virgin space and gives the prose the appearance of a poem or a musical score. Thus the white space materializes silence. Another strategy: the indications of a pause. Agatha multiplies notations which might easily be regarded as didascalia, those instructions provided by the dramaturge to her interpreters and sometimes put in parentheses: "A very long silence," "long silence," "she does not answer," "silence. She gradually remembers." But for Marguerite Duras these indications constitute an integral part of the book, they as much as any of the rest. Does she not lavish this advice upon the reader: "Everything must be read, the empty spaces too"? Empty space, exerting its allure precisely by its emptiness, rich in various interpretations which spur the image-repertoire. And once this has been said, other causes are to be envisaged.

For these silences and these blank spaces have numerous justifications: excess of emotion which reduces the discourse to an interior, inaudible scream, mistrust of a language that has been worn out and is now incapable of restoring the wealth of sensations, an art of sacrifice which neglects the superfluous in order to return the sentence to its essential glory. Topography rather than typography, opening onto the writing of limitless extent.

No More leads us to considerations which complete the foregoing. Anguish inspires the author and triumphs, apparently over her choice of modes of expression. The white spaces are the zero degree of a writing which veers but is not resigned to ending. Hence the frequent expression: "Silence, and then,". She acknowledges emptiness in order to announce that language will fill it—later, some other day, indefinitely. Doubtless too we will be struck by Yann's respect for an oeuvre of which he knows every secret. For it seems highly likely that the appearance of *No More* is his responsibility, since it is he who reports the author's speech. Marguerite Duras would not have rejected it. On November 27, 1994, to the question, "What use is writing?" she answers: "It's a way of keeping still and speaking at the same time." This is the book in which, between the lines, we perceive the temptation to abdicate, vigilance, a respite granted by force to the speech or to the writing which are being exhausted.

The empty fields of this book, deserted by writing, the silence in counterpoint to certain utterances flings them back from the finite toward the infinite, from here below to the divine space where Marguerite Duras places Yann, then praying him to leave it because she is afraid. Less than a year before, she had teased him in this regard: "If there is a God, it's you. You believe in Him as hard as iron, don't you." Concerning his own religious faith Yann says nothing but he conforms to the vocabulary of the liturgical year, mentioning, as we have seen, Palm Sunday, Good Friday and Holy Saturday. One of his first questions on November 22, 1994, concerns paradise. The word makes Marguerite Duras laugh.

Hence we might be tempted to regard her metaphysical anxiety as negligible. *No More* grants her moreover a short allowance, but if we read carefully, the book sustains it in a manner that is fluctuating, temporary, ambiguous, as in previous remarks or texts. On December 25, 1994, and January 6, 1995, implicit reference is made to *Summer Rain* (1990), to its epilogue, when the showers resemble a flood of sobs. We recall that Ernesto, the hero, a child of genius—here a pleonasm, since for this writer childhood and genius are synonyms—discovers a strange book burned on almost every page. The whole narrative is organized around his discovery. Now, this book which Ernesto makes his own includes various extracts taken from the Old Testament, which Marguerite Duras read around the age of eighteen, thanks to a Jewish lover named Freddie, the model for the Vice-Consul who gives his title to the work of 1965.

As for *Summer Rain*, in which her main character serves as a sort of spokesman, the writer suggests that the partially destroyed, hence illegible or virtually incomprehensible book illustrates her own opinion concerning humanity. God is its major problem because nothing allows us to declare that He exists or does not exist. The consequence is that the word God, very frequently employed, designates an irremediable and painful absence which constrains human beings to silence.

Yet by this absence would not God have sought to manifest His presence, a negative presence! This is the sense of a declaration made in 1990, in an allusion to the Arch of La Défense in Paris, in which Marguerite Duras proceeds to say: "The Arch is, I believe, the only religious monument, not only in France but in the whole world. This blank white architecture is the empty Place of God." This notion, close to a certain Judaic tradition based on the logical impossibility of God's presence in the world, which does not imply his non-existence, shows first of all a recurrent feature of the writer's work: her fascination for what she calls "the Jewish thing," and then the spell cast upon her by the splendor of the Biblical verses, so great that much of her style is derived from them. *No More* confirms this double attraction.

Regarding Yann, on July 10, 1995, she utters these words: "You are Yann Andréa Steiner."

Why Steiner, she had been asked upon the publication of the book of which he is the eponymous hero, and had explained: "He's someone very sorrowful, very intelligent, very silent, and childlike too. He might have been a Jew and I have made him a Jew. I have naturally associated him with Steiner. It is a key-word, a word that belongs to me." In this personal conception of Jewishness, we will hold onto the term silent. Pervasively silence and presence, absence and speech exchange their values. Similarly Ernesto scarcely speaks, but when he addresses his family, this taciturn young man echoes the sombre harmonies of the book of Koheleth (Ecclesiastes, according to the Greek terminology) which the Old Testament classifies, after the Torah and the Prophets, in the Ketubim. It is found to be an essential part of the poetic collections. Marguerite Duras quotes lines from it:

> If the rain falls in the sun, a dead sun among the
> cries of children, if happiness seems impossible and
> paradise a deceit, it is because
>> "All is vanity
>> Vanity of vanities
>> and a striving after wind."

For it is difficult to live between a risky proposition: God, and His ill-affirmed negation: not God. This vacillation traverses *No More* from end to end. Apparently certain that nothing remains after death, Marguerite Duras implores, once and then twice, that God to kill her, then she imagines columns reaching heaven. A fleeting hesitation rises in her: "I don't know about God every day."

Less ephemeral are the comparisons she establishes between God and writing. For her, writing has something to do with God, with a sort of very troubled, very troubling premonition of God. The God of Genesis accomplished the Creation by speaking, every writer, by her language which creates life, becomes aware, one day or another, of her demiurgic power. *Le Monde extérieur* (1993) ratifies this point of view. To write is to rival God. In *Les Contemplations,* Victor Hugo exclaimed "For the word is the

Word, and the Word is God." Exceeding the definition, young Aurélia in *Aurélia Steiner* (1979): "the forgetting of God is an equivalent of God." At the heart of a world that has become incompatible with the notion of God, writing attempts to sow the signs of a new version of the sacred. If Marguerite Duras aspires to God, it is only in her books:

> The world exists because the book exists; to exist is to grow with one's name.

In 1943, Marguerite Donnadieu trades her hated surname for the pseudonym Duras. She borrows this name from a large market-town in southwest France near which her father had bought a house she had visited as a child. No one will call her anything but Duras. The word makes her a woman apart: a writer whose activity quickly becomes a tyrannical need, the most lasting of her passions.

On November 21, 1994, to Yann's very first question: "What would you say for yourself," she answers: "Duras." On December 10 he insists: "Who are you? The same answer: "Duras, no more." She returns to the subject on February 10, 1995: "When someone says the word writer to Duras, it has a double weight." On this point, she has never permitted any doubt. Her capacity for invention, her aptitude for assimilating sensations or emotions in order to render their passing aroma, her craving to reveal the whole world: so many factors which impel her to build, on the debris of her daily life, the pulverized and accidental raw material, a stable edifice: the work itself, her oeuvre.

Having freed herself from her initial identity, she chooses another to which she feels herself predestined, the one she prizes: "I am a writer. Nothing else is worth remembering." Moi, Duras . . . Nowhere is she skeptical of her literary vocation. Everything else is secondary. Writing is an urgent summation, a supreme value in which resides, precious and intangible, the image which the author constructs for her own use. If we were to stop there, it might be said that *No More* is tempered by no modesty whatever. Marguerite Duras speaks of herself in the third person, declares herself talented, certain that her work is lasting, herself unquestionably a genius: "You know, that's a confirmation of Duras, everywhere in this world and the next." The next world? Hyperbole is the consciousness of her fame.

Moreover, what meaning would modesty have for someone who has completely, tirelessly, flawlessly dedicated herself to that operation of a tragic nature which is to writing? Her primary goal appears at regular intervals: "To find what to write next," in other words to make a book, a new text. A lacerating, chimerical project and yet an achieved one, since *No More* exists, the work of that oeuvre being constructed before our eyes. Around this project composite thoughts are articulated. They are not out of place among other renewed references to different aspects of her work. Amusingly, she parades her distaste for psychological pablum, indeed absent from her books. Because they are not among those which literary history classifies "analytical novels," hers have nothing to do with the realism of introspection. They find their substance elsewhere, between sleep and waking, in the equivocal. They invite the reader to peer into the dense night of beings and of things, not to delight passively in their deceptive transparence.

And the reader will do so, if he acknowledges that Marguerite Duras does not reject immediacy, spontaneity, for the sake of abstract reflection. Moreover, he must accept that she sides with the greatest subjectivity, not in order to tell stories whose tranquil unfolding he will unthinkingly follow, but in order to lead him into the deepest part of that internalized *maquis* of which the poet René Char speaks, that is, toward her truth as a writer, asserting herself, contesting herself in an uninterrupted quest for herself:

I want nothing
But to speak of myself again, always, like
a monotonous machine-gun. Myself
again and again.

She has explained herself on this subject long before *No More;* she is moved to tears only before herself, before her violence. An unlimited egocentrism? No, a facet of an immense, fragmented self-portrait. It is up to the reader to find others in her works. Here and there it is himself he will discover, thereby uniting with the author in an intimate relationship. Moreover, if Marguerite Duras remains certain of being the wild and inspired writer, she does not conceal what shackles and undermines that conviction. That she can no longer write to destroy herself is now significant. Try as she will to force herself to live, hence to write, what dismays her, in this last book, is a closed sluice against which the flood of words breaks, a dike separating her from what she was and transforming her without her ceasing to be herself. And again, a denial, a wall raised before her former self-assurance:

I know something about language.
That's something I'm really good at.

And on the other hand, when she adds:

> All my life I've written.
> Like a sausage out of the grinder,
> that's what I've done.

she reverts to *Emily L.:* "It takes imbecility to begin to believe it's possible . . . You begin. And then it happens, you write, you continue. And then there it is, it's done." Self-denigration, against which nothing rebels within her, is the painful other side of her love for writing. As solid as this love is, with utter familiarity, she frequently explains it as fatality, a kind of accepted bondage, by the extreme facility of her pen, and derides herself for it. *No More* amplifies the doubts after unwonted bursts of enthusiasm. An unforeseen reversal flings her to the antipodes of her fervent faith in writing, and she becomes sadly incredulous. No, writing does not lead to salvation, it saves nothing. By turns exalted, dissolved in silence, reborn, it seems no more than betrayal, a fallacious barricade erected against death.

Intermittently, several pages attest that the desire to write resists. Yet the passage to the act of writing seems aleatory. It is summarized in one explicit title: *Le Livre à disparaître,* as explicit as *No More,* lugubrious refrain of a mourning cantilena.

This death in a book consorts with a death by the book: is it not the book which on February 19, 1996, demands in its turn the death of its author, Duras? Extravagant demand? Delirium? Perhaps, but what a symbol! The departure of the writing and of the writer for a higher level or nowhere, far from dividing them, links them, as in life, to a single and unique destiny.

While the fires of death dance in the night, the chiaroscuro of the mind has more to say than any learned commentary: there is no more Duras because there is nothing more to write. The work has devoured the life which puts an end to the work in a perfect coincidence.

No More closes on an image of Apocalypse and abandons to the reader its rhapsodic prose, all fragments and rapid variations, like the shattered glass at the bottom of a kaleidoscope. A prose as melancholy as a season's end, as troubling as art brut, as simple and abrupt as grief.

Christiane Blot-Labarrère

CHRISTIANE BLOT-LABARRÉRE is among the very few whose writings were respected by Duras.

C'est Tout

Pour Yann.
On ne sait jamais, avant,
ce qu'on écrit.
Dépêche-toi de penser à moi.

Pour Yann mon amant de la nuit.
Signé: Marguerite, l'aimante de cet amant adoré,
le 20 novembre 1994, Paris, rue Saint-Benoît.

Le 21 novembre, l'après-midi, rue Saint-Benoît.

Y.A.: Que diriez-vous de vous-même?
M.D.: Duras.
Y.A.: Que diriez-vous de moi?
M.D.: Indéchiffrable.

Plus tard, le même après-midi.

Quelquefois je suis vide pendant très longtemps.
Je suis sans identité.
Ça fait peur d'abord. Et puis ça passe par un
mouvement de bonheur. Et puis ça s'arrête.
Le bonheur, c'est-à-dire morte un peu.
Un peu absente du lieu où je parle.

Plus tard, encore.

C'est une question de temps. Je ferai un livre.
Je voudrais mais ça n'est pas sûr que j'écrive ce livre.
C'est aléatoire.

Le 22 novembre, l'après-midi, rue Saint-Benoît.

Y.A.: Vous avez peur de la mort?
M.D.: Je ne sais pas. Je ne sais pas répondre. Je
ne sais plus rien depuis que je suis arrivée à la
mer.
Y.A.: Et avec moi ?
M.D.: Avant et maintenant c'est l'amour entre
toi et moi. La mort et l'amour. Ce sera ce que tu
voudras, toi, que tu sois.
Y.A.: Votre définition de vous?
M.D.: Je ne suis pas, comme en ce moment: je ne
sais pas quoi écrire.
Y.A.: Votre livre préféré absolument?
M.D.: *Le Barrage,* l'enfance.

Y.A.: Et le paradis, vous irez?
M.D.: Non. Ça me fait rire.
Y.A.: Pourquoi?
M.D.: Je ne sais pas. Je n'y crois pas du tout.
Y.A.: Et après la mort, qu'est-ce qui reste?
M.D.: Rien. Que les vivants
qui se sourient, qui se souviennent.
Y.A.: Qui va se souvenir de vous?
M.D.: Les jeunes lecteurs. Les petits élèves.

Y.A.: Vous vous préoccupez de quoi?
M.D.: D'écrire. Une occupation tragique, c'est-à-

dire relative au courant de la vie. Je suis dedans sans effort.

Plus tard, le même après-midi.

Y.A.: Vous avez un titre pour le prochain livre?
M.D.: Oui. Le livre à disparaître.

Le 23 novembre à Paris, 15 heures.

Je veux parler de quelqu'un.
D'un homme de vingt-cinq ans tout au plus.
C'est un homme très beau qui veut mourir avant
d'être repéré par la mort.
Vous l'aimiez.
Plus que ça.

La beauté de ses mains,
c'est ça, oui.
Ses mains qui avancent avec la colline—devenue distincte,
claire, aussi lumineuse qu'une grâce d'enfant.
Je vous embrasse.
Je vous attends comme j'attends celui qui détruira cette grâce
défaite, douce et encore chaude.
A toi donnée, entière, de tout mon corps, cette grâce.

Plus tard dans te même après-midi.

J'ai voulu vous dire
que je vous aimais.
Le crier.
C'est tout.

Rue Saint-Benoît, le dimanche 27 novembre.

Etre ensemble c'est l'amour, la mort, la parole,
dormir.

Plus tard, ce dimanche.

Y.A.: Vous diriez quoi de vous?
M.D.: Je ne sais plus très bien qui je suis.
Je suis avec mon amant.
Le nom, je ne sais pas.
Ce n'est pas important.
Etre ensemble comme avec un amant.
J'aurais voulu que ça m'arrive.
Etre ensemble avec un amant.

Silence, et puis.

Y.A.: Ça sert à quoi, écrire?
M.D.: C'est à la fois se taire et parler. Ecrire. Ça
veut dire aussi chanter quelquefois.
Y.A.: Danser?
M.D.: Ça compte aussi. C'est un état de l'individu, danser.
J'ai beaucoup aimé danser.
Y.A.: Pourquoi?
M.D.: Je ne sais pas encore.

Silence, et puis.

Y.A.: Etes-vous très douée?
M.D.: Oui. Il me semble bien.

Ecrire c'est très près du rythme de la parole.

Lundi 28 novembre, 75 heures, rue Saint-Benoît.

Il faut parler de l'homme de *La Maladie de la Mort.*
Qui est-ce?
Comment en est-il arrivé là?

Ecrire sur la maigreur,
à partir de la maigreur de l'homme.

Un autre jour.

Il n'est plus apparu dans la chambre.
Jamais.
C'était inutile d'attendre son chant, parfois rieur,
parfois triste, parfois morne.
Très vite il est redevenu l'oiseau que j'avais
connu dans les champs.

Plus tard, ce même autre jour.

Faire savoir à Yann que ce n'est pas lui qui écrit
les lettres, mais qu'il pourra signer la dernière.
Ça me fera profondément plaisir. Signé: Duras.

Plus tard encore.

Le nom chinois de mon amant.
Je ne lui ai jamais parlé dans sa langue.

Un autre jour, rue Saint-Benoît.

Pour Yann.
Pour rien.
Le ciel est vide.
Ça fait des années que j'aime cet homme.
Un homme que je n'ai pas encore nommé.
Un homme que j'aime.
Un homme qui me quittera.
Le reste, devant, derrière moi, avant et après
moi, ça m'indiffère.
Je t'aime.

Toi, tu ne peux plus prononcer le nom que je
porte et donné par les parents.
Des amants inconnus.
Laissons faire si tu veux.
Encore pour quelques jours d'attente.
Tu me demandes attente de quoi, je réponds: je
ne sais pas.
Attendre.
Dans le devenir du vent.
Peut-être demain je t'écrirai encore.

On peut vivre de ça.

Rire et pleurer ensuite.
Je parle du temps qui sourd de la terre.
Je n'ai plus de souffle.
Il faut que je m'arrête de parler.

Plus tard.

Des activités diverses qui me tentent de temps en temps, par exemple la mort de ce jeune homme. Je ne sais plus comment il s'appelle, comment l'appeler. Littéralement son insignifiance est grande.

Silence, et puis.

Je n'ai plus aucune notion sur ce que je croyais savoir ou attendre de revoir.
Voilà, c'est tout.

Silence, et puis.

Le commencement de la fin de cet amour effectivement effrayant, avec le regret de chaque heure.

Et puis il y a eu l'heure qui a suivi, incompréhensible, sortant du fond du temps.

Heure horrible.

Superbe et horrible.

Je suis arrivée à ne pas me tuer rien qu'à l'idée de sa mort.

De sa mort et de sa vie.

Silence, et puis.

Je n'ai pas dit le principal sur sa personne, son âme, ses pieds, ses mains, son rire.

Le principal pour moi, c'est de laisser son regard quand il est seul. Quand il est dans le désordre de la pensée.

Il est très beau. C'est difficile à savoir.

Si je commence à parler de lui, je ne m'arrête plus.

Ma vie est comme incertaine, plus incertaine, oui, que la sienne à lui devant moi.

Silence, et puis.

Je voudrais continuer à divaguer comme je le fais par certains après-midi d'été comme celui-là.

Je n'en ai plus le goût ni le courage.

Le 14 octobre 1994.

Le 14 octobre 1914. Le titre ici ne signifie rien que pour
l'auteur. Le titre ne veut donc rien dire. Le titre aussi attend
ça: un titre. Un ciment.
Je suis au bord de la date fatale.
Elle est NULLE.
Pourtant la date est inscrite sur du papier blond. Elle a été
inscrite par une tête blonde d'homme. Une tête d'enfant.
Moi, je crois cela: je crois par-dessus moi ce qui a été écrit
parallèlement à cette tête d'enfant. C'est le RESTE de l'écrit.
C'est un sens de l'écrit.
C'est aussi la senteur d'un amour qui passait par là, par
l'enfant.
Un amour sans direction qui avait senti la chair d'un enfant
qui se mourait de lire l'inconnu du désir.
Le tout s'évanouira quand s'effacera le texte de la lecture.

Le 15 octobre.

Je suis en contact avec moi-même dans une liberté qui
coïncide avec moi.

Silence, et puis.

Je n'ai jamais eu de modèle.
Je désobéissais en obéissant.
Quand j'écris je suis de la même folie que dans la vie. Je rejoins
des masses de pierre quand j'écris. Les pierres du Barrage.

Samedi 10 décembre, 15 heures, rue Saint-Benoît.

Vous y allez tout droit à la solitude.
Moi, non, j'ai les livres.

Silence, et puis.

Je me sens perdue.
Mort c'est équivalent.
C'est terrifiant.
Je n'ai plus envie de faire l'effort.
Je ne pense à personne.
C'est terminé le reste.
Vous aussi.
Je suis seule.

Silence, et puis.

Ce n'est plus du malheur que tu vis, c'est le désespoir.

Silence, et puis.

Y.A.: Vous êtes qui?
M.D.: Duras, c'est tout.
Y.A.: Elle fait quoi, Duras?
M.D.: Elle fait la littérature.

Silence, et puis.

Trouver quoi écrire encore.

Paris le 25 décembre 1994.

La pluie des enfants est tombée dans le soleil.
Avec le bonheur.
Je suis allée voir.
Après il a fallu leur expliquer que c'était normal.
Depuis des siècles. Parce que les enfants ils ne
comprenaient pas, ils ne pouvaient pas encore comprendre
l'intelligence des Dieux.

Après il a fallu continuer à marcher dans la forêt.
Et chanter avec les adultes, les chiens, les chats.

Paris, le 28 décembre.

Une lettre pour moi.
Il suffirait de changer ou de laisser sans devenir aucun.
La lettre.

Le 31 décembre 1994.

Bonne année à Yann Andréa.
Je m'ennuie de tes lettres courtes.

Le 3 janvier, rue Saint-Benoît.

Yann, je suis encore là.
Il faut que je parte.
Je ne sais plus où me mettre.
Je vous écris comme si je vous appelais.
Peut-être pourriez-vous me voir.
Je sais que ça ne servira à rien.

Le 6 janvier.

Yann.
J'espère te voir à la fin de l'après-midi.
De tout mon cœur.
De tout mon cœur.

Le 10 février.

Une intelligence en allée de soi.
Comme évadée.
Quand on dit le mot écrivain à Duras, ça fait un
double poids.
Je suis l'écrivain sauvage et inespérée.

Plus tard, le même après-midi.

Vanité des vanités.
Tout est vanité et poursuite du vent.
Ces deux phrases donnent toute la littérature de la terre.
Vanité des vanités, oui.
Ces deux phrases à elles seules ouvrent le monde: les choses,
les vents, les cris des enfants, le soleil mort pendant ces cris.
Que le monde aille à sa perte.
Vanité des vanités.

Tout est vanité et poursuite du vent.

Le 3 mars.

C'est moi la poursuite du vent.

Silence, et puis.

Il y a des papiers que je dois ranger à l'ombre de mon
intelligence.
C'est indélébile ce que je fais.

Samedi 25 mars.

Je suis peinée que les décennies passent si vite.
Mais je suis quand même de ce côté-là du
monde.
C'est tellement dur de mourir.
A un certain moment de la vie, les choses sont
finies.
Je le sens comme ça: les choses sont finies.
C'est comme ça.

Silence, et puis.

Je vous aimerai jusqu'à ma mort.
Je vais essayer de ne pas mourir trop tôt.
C'est tout ce que j'ai à faire.

Silence, et fuis.

Yann, tu ne te sens pas un peu le pendentif de
Duras?

Vendredi saint.

Prends-moi dans tes larmes, dans tes rires, dans
tes pleurs.

Samedi saint.

Ce que je vais devenir.
J'ai peur.
Viens.
Venez avec moi.

Vite, venez.

Plus tard, le même après-midi.

Allons voir l'horreur, la mort.

Plus tard encore.

Caressez-moi.
Venez dans mon visage avec moi.
Vite, venez.

Silence, et puis.

Je t'aime trop.
Je ne sais plus écrire.
L'amour trop grand entre nous, jusqu'à l'horreur.

Silence, et puis.

Je ne sais pas où je vais.
J'ai peur.
Partons ensemble sur la route.
Viens vite.
Je vais t'envoyer des lettres.
C'est tout.
Ça fait peur d'écrire.
Y'a des trucs comme ça qui me font peur.

Dimanche 9 avril. Les Rameaux.

On est tous les deux des innocents.

Silence, et puis.

J'ai une vie maigre maintenant.
Pauvre.
Je suis devenue pauvre.
Je vais écrire un texte nouveau. Sans homme. Il
n'y aura plus rien.
Je suis presque plus rien.
Je ne vois plus rien.
C'est encore le tout, longtemps, avant la mort.

Plus tard.

Il n'y a pas de dernier baiser.

Plus tard encore.

Il ne faut pas vous en faire pour le fric.
C'est tout.
Je n'ai plus rien à dire.
Pas même un mot.
Rien à dire.
Allons faire cent mètres sur la route.

Ce même dimanche.

S'il y a un bon Dieu, c'est toi. Tu y crois dur
comme fer, toi.

Silence, et puis.

Moi, je peux tout recommencer.
Dès demain.

A tout moment.
Je recommence un livre.
J'écris.
Et hop, voilà?
Moi, le langage, je connais.
Je suis très forte là-dedans.

Silence, et puis.

Dites donc, ça se confirme Duras, partout dans le monde et au-delà.

Le mercredi 12 avril, après-midi, rue Saint-Benoît.

Viens.
Viens dans le soleil, quel qu'il soit.

Le 13 avril.

Toute une vie j'ai écrit.
Comme une andouille, j'ai fait ça.
C'est pas mal non plus d'être comme ça.

Je n'ai jamais été prétentieuse.
Ecrire toute sa vie, ça apprend à écrire. Ça ne sauve de rien.

Le mercredi 19 avril, 15 heures, rue Saint-Benoît.

Il se trouve que j'ai du génie.
J'y suis habituée maintenant.

Silence, et puis.

Je suis un bout de bois blanc.
Et vous aussi.
D'une autre couleur.

Le 11 juin.

Vous êtes ce que vous êtes et ça m'enchante.

Silence, et puis.

Venez vite.
Vite, donnez-moi un peu de votre force.
Venez dans mon visage.

Le 28 juin.

Le mot amour existe.

Le 3 juillet, 15 heures, Neauphle-le-Château.

Je sais bien que tu as d'autres ambitions. Je sais bien que tu
es triste. Mais ça m'est égal. Que tu m'aimes, c'est le plus
important. Le reste m'est égal. Je m'en fous.

Plus tard, le même après-midi.

Je me sens écrasée d'exister.
Ça me donne envie d'écrire.
J'ai écrit très fort sur toi quand tu étais parti—sur l'homme que
j'aime.
Tu es dans le charme le plus vif que j'aie jamais vu.
Tu es l'auteur de tout.

Tout ce que j'ai fait tu aurais pu le faire.
Je t'entends dire que tu as renoncé à cette phrase, cette phrase-là.

Silence, et puis.

Est-ce que tu entends ce silence.
Moi, j'entends les phrases que tu as dites à la
place de celle-là qui écrit.

Silence, et puis.

Tout a été écrit par toi, par ce corps que tu as. Je vais arrêter là
ce texte pour en prendre un autre de toi, fait pour toi, fait à ta
place.

Silence, et puis.

Alors, ce serait quoi, ce que tu veux entendre
écrire?

Silence, et puis.

Je ne supporte pas ton devenir.

Le 4 juillet à Neauphle.

Comme une peur immédiate de la mort.
Et après une fatigue immense.

Silence, et puis.

Viens.
Il faut qu'on parle de notre amour.
On va trouver les mots pour ça.
Il n'y aurait pas de mots peut-être.

Silence, et puis.

J'aime la vie, même comme elle est là.
C'est bien, j'ai trouvé les mots.

Plus tard, le même jour.

Dans l'avenir je ne veux rien.
Que parler de moi encore, toujours, comme une
plate-forme monotone. Encore de moi.

Silence, et puis.

Moi, je veux que ça disparaisse ou que Dieu me tue.

Silence, et puis.

Viens vite.
Je vais mieux.
La peur est moins solide.
Laisse-moi là où je suis avec la peur de la mort de ma mère,
restée intacte, entière.
C'est tout.

Samedi 8 juillet, 14 heures, à Neauphle.

Je n'ai plus rien dans la tête.

Que des choses vides.

Silence, et puis.

Ça y est.
Je suis morte.
C'est fini.

Silence, et puis.

Ce soir on va manger quelque chose de très fort.
Un plat chinois par exemple. Un plat de la Chine détruite.

Le 10 juillet à Neauphle.

Vous devenez beau.
Je vous regarde.
Vous êtes Yann Andréa Steiner.

Le 20 juillet, Neauphle, l'après-midi.

Les baisers de vous, j'y crois jusqu'à la fin de ma vie.

Au revoir.
Au revoir à personne. Même pas à vous. C'est fini.
Il n'y a rien.
Il faut fermer la page.
Viens maintenant.
Il faut y aller.

Temps. Silence, et puis.

Il serait temps que vous fassiez quelque chose. Vous ne pouvez pas rester à rien faire. Ecrire peut-être.

Silence, et puis.

Comment faire pour vivre un peu, encore un peu.
C'est tout.
C'est plus moi maintenant. C'est quelqu'un que
je ne connais plus.

Silence, et puis.

Tu peux maintenant ouvrir ton cœur. C'est moi peut-être. Je ne suis pas perdue pour toi.

Silence, et puis.

Pour adoucir la vie?
Personne ne le sait. Il faut essayer de vivre. Il ne faut pas se jeter dans la mort.
C'est tout.
C'est tout ce que j'ai à dire.

Le 21 juillet.

Viens.

Je n'aime rien.

Je viendrais autour de toi.
Viens à côté de moi.
C'est tout.

Je veux être à l'abri de ça.
Viens vite me mettre quelque part.

Plus tard dans l'après-midi.

Je ne peux plus du tout tenir.
Je ne crois pas qu'on puisse nommer cette peur.
Pas encore.

Donne-moi ta bouche.
Viens vite pour aller plus vite.
Vite.
C'est tout.
Vite.

Samedi 22 juillet. Pluie.

Je ne ferai plus rien pour restreindre ou pour
agrandir ta vie.

Silence.

Viens dans mon visage.

Silence.

Je vous aimerai jusqu'à ne pas vous abandonner.

Silence.

Vous êtes nul. Rien. Un double zéro.

Dimanche 23 juillet.

Je ne peux me résoudre à être rien.

Silence.

Ne pas pouvoir être comme toi, c'est un truc que je regrette.

Silence.

Venez avec moi dans le grand lit et on attendra.
Rien.

Silence.

Je suis glacée par la folie.

Y.A.: Vous voulez ajouter quelque chose?
M.D.: Je ne sais pas ajouter. Je sais seulement créer. Seulement
ça.

Lundi 24 juillet.

Venez m'aimer.
Venez.
Viens dans ce papier blanc.
Avec moi.

Je te donne ma peau.
Viens.
Vite.

Dis-moi au revoir.
C'est tout.
Je ne sais plus rien de toi.

Je m'en vais avec les algues.
Viens avec moi.

Le 31 juillet.

Quelle est ma vérité à moi?
Si tu la connais, dis-la-moi.
Je suis perdue.

Regarde-moi.

Le 1er août, l'après-midi.

Je crois que c'est terminé. Que ma vie c'est fini.
Je ne suis plus rien.
Je suis devenue complètement effrayante.
Je ne tiens plus ensemble.
Viens vite.
Je n'ai plus de bouche, plus de visage.

Paris, le 12 octobre 95.

Viens dans ma vie.

15 h 30.

Je suis morte. C'est fini.

Mardi 31 octobre.

Il n'y a plus de Duras. Je ne peux plus rien. Je n'ai plus rien.

17 heures.

Je suis une aimante.
Tu es un aimant.

Vendredi 3 novembre.

Tu as demandé à Dieu pour qu'il me tue?

16 heures.

Il faudrait que j'aie le courage de mourir.

jeudi 16 novembre.

Le long de la mer. Le long de toi.

Je ne suis plus rien. Je ne sais plus où je suis.
C'est fini.

Des colonnes pour se rapprocher du ciel.
Viens.

18 novembre.

Je suis morte. C'est fini. Après ça sera dur pour vous.

Mercredi 22 novembre.

Je deviens folle parce que je n'ai plus rien.
Je crois que c'est fini, ma vie.
Ma bouche est fatiguée. Il n'y a plus de mots.
Je n'ai plus rien. Plus de papier.

Le 2 décembre.

C'est fini. Je n'ai plus rien. Je n'ai plus de bouche, plus de visage.
C'est atroce.

Mercredi 6 décembre.

Vous êtes un vieux corbeau. Un vieux salaud.

Jeudi 7 décembre.

Vous avez une force dans le visage.

Vendredi 8 décembre.

Vous êtes une grande casserole de connards.
Vous êtes tous complètement foutus.
Tout est insupportable.

19 heures.

Y.A.: Qu'est-ce que vous sentez?
M.D.: L'état de mort qui vient.
C'est fini. Tout est fini. C'est comme ça.

Le 24 décembre.

Je ne mange pas parce que je n'ai plus rien de la vie.
Regarde: mes mains sont mortes.

Mardi 26 décembre.

J'ai horreur des mangeailles psychologiques.
C'est dégoûtant.

Minuit.

Je ne veux rien, rien qui soit conditionné.
Je veux un café, et tout de suite.

Le 27 décembre.

Regardez-moi: je suis vide. C'est la quiétude qui me manque.

Le 28 décembre.

Arrêtez de faire le tintin.

Le 29 décembre.

Je n'ai plus rien. Je suis morte. Je le sens.
Apportez-moi une boîte.

J'ai envie de voir ma mère.

Dépêchez-vous.

J'ai tout le corps qui me flambe.

Plus tard

La perte de votre cœur, ça vous fait mal?

Plus tard

Viens vite me voir, avec moi, donne-moi quelque chose.

Samedi 30 décembre, 2 h 30 dans la nuit;

Vous êtes séparé du royaume de Duras.

Mercredi 3 janvier 96.

Le vide, c'est-à-dire la liberté.
Les femmes closes ne disent rien. Elles attendent.
Une femme seule ne parle pas.

Samedi 6 janvier.

Ce n'est pas grand chose la gentillesse. Ce qui importe c'est la pensée extrême qui ne mène nulle part, à rien.

Plus tard

La haine, ça sert à tenir.

Le 7 janvier.

Je n'ai plus rien dans la tête. Je le sais.

Le 8 janvier.

Je n'ai rien d'autre à faire qu'à m'en aller.
Je ne sais pas où.

J'ai fait du feu et tout était blanc.

Je ne perçois aucun sens—et ça me rend seule,
pas triste, non, seule.

Je vois des gants noirs près de moi.

Plus tard

Et elle vient d'où cette littérature?
J'aime les livres ouverts.

Venez dans la salle blanche. Venez m'enlever
une robe de soie. Je n'ai plus rien à porter.

C'est une vie magnifique que je t'ai fait ouvrir. Ça n'a pas de
sens, mais à la fin, on y croit.

Je n'ai jamais oublié un livre.

On est seul pour personne. Une misère pauvre. Une pauvre
femme pauvre. Ce que je suis. Et c'est tout.

Ne me laissez pas tomber, je vous en supplie.
Je pleure au fond de moi.
Laissez-moi, je suis quelqu'un de libre.

Jeudi 18 janvier.

Ma main, elle écrit.

Le 19 janvier.

Une douleur confidentielle.

Yann, il faudrait que je t'excuse, je ne sais pas de quoi.
Je suis belle. Carrément, fortement belle.

Le 25 janvier.

C'est la fin. C'est fini. C'est la mort. C'est l'horreur.
Ça m'ennuie de mourir.

Je sens un rien qui arrive: la mort. Et ça fait peur.

Il y a des yeux éteints.
J'ai très peur.
Vite.
Je ne crois pas. Je crois que je suis dans le cirage.

Il n'y a rien. Tout ce que l'on fait, il n'y a rien.
Je ne peux pas écrire les choses qui m'abattent.
J'aime toujours ma mère. Y a rien à faire, je
l'aime toujours.

Vous ne pouvez jamais rien comprendre, c'est une sorte de
déficience. Moi, je comprends un peu.

Une page, vite. Et on arrive. Et on arrête. Vite.

Yann, je t'ai tellement aimé. Et maintenant il faut que je
m'éloigne.

Je ne sais pas pour le Bon Dieu tous les jours . . . On dépend de pas grand chose. Et après on voit. Tous les cinq jours peut-être?

Vendredi 26 janvier.

Pendant quelques secondes j'ai senti la senteur de la terre.

Yann, sors de cet espace divin, ça fait peur. Tu fais peur quelquefois.

J'en ai marre d'être seule. Je vais prendre un type pour travailler sur le travail.

Je voudrais faire un livre sur moi et sur ce que je pense. C'est tout. N'importe quoi de noir et de blanc.

Vous êtes très creux. Moi, j'ai toujours été dans les fonds.

Le 29 janvier.

Le vide. Le vide devant moi.

Mardi 30 janvier.

Ce que je sais c'est que je n'ai plus rien. C'est l'horreur. Il n'y a plus que le vide. Les vides. Ce vide du dernier terrain.
On n'est pas deux. On est seul chacun.

Le 31 janvier.

Laissez-moi. C'est fini. Laissez-moi mourir. J'ai honte.

Vendredi 2 février.

Tu te souviens comme on a été beau. Plus personne après n'a été beau comme ça.

Le 15 février.

La chambre ancienne où l'on s'aimait.

Le 16 février.

C'est curieux comme je t'aime toujours, même quand je ne t'aime pas.

Lundi 19 février.

Je sais ce que je vais subir: la mort. Ce qui m'attend: ma figure à la morgue. C'est horrible, je ne veux pas.

Plus tard

Tous ces gens qui demandent la mort de Duras.

Plus tard

Il n'y a pas que la honte, la honte de tout.
Je ne suis plus rien.
Plus rien.
Je ne sais plus être.
Ce qui n'est pas fini, c'est l'argument de votre personne.

Plus tard

Il y a le livre qui demande ma mort.
Y.A.: Qui est l'auteur.
M.D.: Moi. Duras.

Mardi 20 février.

Yann, il faut que je vous demande pardon, pardon pour tout.

Le 26 février.

Je vous ai connu très fort.
Je vais partir vers un autre degré.
Nulle part.

Le 28 février.

C'est fini.
Tout est fini.
C'est l'horreur.

Le jeudi 29 février, 13 h.

Je vous aime.
Au revoir.

POSTFACE

C'est vers la fin du mois d'août 1995 que Yann Andréa m'a apporté le début de *C'est Tout:* quelques feuillets dactylographiés qui allaient du 20 novembre 1994 au 1er août 1995. Nous les avons publiés très vite et Marguerite Duras a pu voir le livre. Tout le monde savait alors qu'elle n'allait pas bien. Puis quelques jours après sa mort, le 3 mars 1996, Yann m'a donné ceux qui s'arrêtent au 29 février. Qu'il s'agisse de notes écrites par elle, ou retranscrites par Yann, ce qui frappe, pour qui a connu Marguerite Duras vers la fin de sa vie, c'est à quel point on y retrouve sa voix, cette manière déraisonnable et puissante de contraindre la langue à sa pensée, une manière ici devenue lapidaire, à cause de l'urgence et de la peur du silence. Elle parlait exactement comme elle écrivait, ou l'inverse. C'est pour ce qu'elles disent et c'est aussi pour la volonté de dire jusqu'au bout que j'ai trouvé ces pages mal tapées sur la vieille machine même pas électrique si bouleversantes. Et encore parce que toute l'oeuvre s'y trouve présente, par fragments, par éclairs, échos, comme toujours reprise et revisitée, cette fois ultime, la vraie dernière fois.

—Paul Otchakovsky-Laurens